THE GREEK
WEDDING
SHE NEVER HAD

THE GREEK WEDDING SHE NEVER HAD

CHANTELLE SHAW

MILLS & BOON

First published in Great Britain 2021
by Mills & Boon, an imprint of HarperCollins*Publishers* Ltd,
1 London Bridge Street, London, SE1 9GF

www.harpercollins.co.uk

HarperCollins*Publishers*
1st Floor, Watermarque Building,
Ringsend Road, Dublin 4, Ireland

Large Print edition 2021

The Greek Wedding She Never Had © 2021 Chantelle Shaw

ISBN: 978-0-263-28874-2

07/21

MIX
Paper from
responsible sources
FSC
www.fsc.org
FSC™ C007454

FALKIRK COUNCIL LIBRARIES

Printed and bound in Great Britain
by CPI Group (UK) Ltd, Croydon, CR0 4YY

For Oly,
who will find his own solutions!

PROLOGUE

A SHAFT OF evening sunlight slanting through the window struck the enormous diamond on Eleanor's finger. Set on a platinum band, the square diamond sparkled with fiery brilliance as she held her hand out in front of her to admire the ring. Earlier in the day she'd gasped when Jace had opened a small velvet box to reveal an engagement ring.

They had been walking beside the Seine in Paris when he'd halted and turned to her. 'Will you do me the honour of becoming my wife, *pouláki mou*?' he had asked her softly.

For a few seconds Eleanor had been too shocked to reply, wondering if she had misunderstood him. Jace Zagorakis was a gorgeous Greek god and it seemed impossible that he had proposed marriage to *her*—ordinary Eleanor Buchanan. It was the stuff of fairy tales.

'Do you really want to marry me?' she'd stammered.

'I do.' His sexy smile had sent her heart shooting towards the stratosphere.

'In that case, *yes*,' she'd said joyfully, blinking back tears of happiness as he slid the ring onto her finger. 'Oh, Jace, I love you so much,' she'd murmured when he drew her into his arms. 'Of course I'll marry you.'

'Good.' There had been satisfaction in his voice before he'd claimed her lips in a kiss that left her breathless. 'I would prefer a small wedding as soon as it can be arranged. There is no reason to wait and I am impatient to make you my bride.'

Eleanor had felt as if she were walking on air when they'd spent the afternoon strolling through the Tuileries Garden before heading back to their hotel in sight of the Eiffel Tower. She had returned to her own room to change for dinner.

Now she used the key card Jace had given her and entered his suite. There was no sign of him, but she was early and perhaps he was still dressing, or in the shower. Heat spread over her face as her imagination ran riot, fuelled by memories of his powerfully muscular physique when he had worn a pair of swim shorts on a yacht cruising around the northern Aegean islands two months ago.

Eleanor had been wildly attracted to him on the cruise and over the course of the following weeks, when he had flown to England from his home in Thessaloniki regularly to visit her, she had fallen in love with him. Incredibly, it seemed that Jace shared her feelings.

Crossing the lounge, she saw that the dining table was laid for an intimate dinner. There was a bottle of champagne on ice and a centrepiece of exquisite red roses. The flowers' heady perfume filled the air. Red roses for love. Eleanor's heart skipped a beat at the thought that Jace must have ordered the roses when he'd arranged for a celebration dinner to be served in his suite.

She placed the box of Greek pastries that she'd ordered, knowing they were his favourite, on the table. This was her first visit to Paris. When they had arrived that morning, before taking her sightseeing Jace had led her to a Greek café where they had been served tiny cups of strong black coffee and honey cakes. Eleanor had been amused to discover that ultra-sophisticated and frankly enigmatic business tycoon Jace Zagorakis had a weakness for sweet pastries.There were many more things she had yet to learn about her future husband, she mused. No doubt her grandfather would have advised against rushing into marriage after a whirlwind romance. But Kostas had died six months ago and, although Eleanor missed him, she felt a sense of freedom that she had not experienced while Pappoús had been the head of the family. Not that there were many members of her family left. Just her brother and sister, who resented that Kostas had named her his heir to the hotel business, Gilpin Leisure.

With a faint sigh, Eleanor dismissed thoughts of her problematic siblings. Today was the most wonderful day of her life and she was cocooned in a bubble of happiness. Glancing across the room, she saw through an open door a bedroom with a four-poster bed. Her heart gave a lurch of nervous anticipation. Tonight she planned to sleep with Jace, but it would be her first sexual experience. He was unaware that she was a virgin and she hoped he would not be disappointed.

When he kissed her the passion between them was electrifying, she reminded herself. Jace had awoken her desires, but he had been patient and not rushed her into sex. Now, though, she was eager to give herself to him and show her love for him with her body as well as her heart.

The prospect of losing her virginity did not worry Eleanor, but her old insecurities surfaced at the idea of being naked in front of Jace. He was bound to notice the scar on her back. It ran from the base of her neck all the way down her spine, the result of an operation when she was thirteen to correct a curvature of her spine. The condition, called scoliosis, had required surgery, where two titanium rods and numerous screws had been inserted in her back.

The surgery had been successful but she'd struggled with body image issues, especially when she had started dating, and a boyfriend had reacted with horror to her scar. Self-consciousness about her body was one reason why she had avoided serious relationships.

Jace had broken through her reserve, but on the boat in Greece she'd worn a high-neck swimsuit or covered up with a sarong.

Her pulse leapt when she heard his gravelly, accented voice. The voile curtain across the open glass doors moved in the breeze and she glimpsed his tall figure standing on the suite's private balcony. He was holding his phone in front of him and Eleanor realised that he was on a video call.

'Takis, did you receive my message?'

'I certainly did,' replied a disembodied male voice. 'I assume the announcement that you are engaged is a joke, seeing how you have always maintained that you are a die-hard bachelor with an aversion to marriage.'

'The situation is not as it seems,' Jace drawled.

Eleanor had started to walk back across the room, intending to wait out in the corridor until Jace had finished his conversation. But she hesitated, puzzled by his cynical tone. The two men were talking in Greek, which she spoke fluently, having been taught it by her grandfather.

'So, you are actually engaged to Eleanor

Buchanan.' The man on the phone, Takis, sounded shocked. 'Even though she is the granddaughter of Kostas Pangalos, who you despised when he was alive.'

'My hatred of Kostas has not lessened since his death,' Jace said in a harsh voice that Eleanor had never heard from him before.

She felt a sensation like an ice cube sliding down her spine. Her conscience urged her to leave. Jace wasn't expecting her to arrive for another ten minutes and she should respect his privacy. But her feet were welded to the floor when Takis spoke again.

'For years you've told me how Kostas swindled your father out of his share of their hotel, and Dimitri was financially ruined. So why on earth would you marry your enemy's granddaughter?' Takis sounded incredulous.

'You know I tried to buy the Pangalos, before Kostas died, but he rejected my offer. When I heard that he'd left Eleanor in charge of Gilpin Leisure, I did not know if she was aware of the feud that had existed between my father and her grandfather,' Jace said in a grim tone. 'That's why I asked you to approach her and try to persuade her to sell the Pangalos hotel.'

'Having met Eleanor, I'll admit I'm surprised by your choice of bride,' Takis murmured. 'I mean she is charming and pretty in an understated way, but she's not the sex bomb type you usually go for. Her party-loving sister, on the other hand, is stunning, from photos I've seen of her in the media.'

Jace laughed, but it wasn't his warm, sensual laugh that had attracted Eleanor to him when she'd first met him in Greece. He sounded cold and cynical.

'It's true that Eleanor is not an eye-catching peacock like her showy sister. She is more of an unremarkable sparrow. But my engagement to her is not a love-match.'

Eleanor gave a choked cry. She felt numb with shock and it was as if her lungs were being crushed in a vice, making it agony to breathe. Jace often called her *pouláki mou,* which in English meant 'my little bird'. She had believed that his pet name for her was a sign of his affection. But he had compared her to a boring brown sparrow! As if that wasn't hurtful enough, he evidently thought her sister Lissa was attractive.

The pain in Eleanor's chest felt as though an arrow had pierced her heart. Jace *loved* her, she assured herself frantically. Why else would he have asked her to marry him?

But he hadn't actually said how he felt about her.

Doubt slid like a poisonous serpent into her head as she acknowledged that he had never uttered the three little words she longed to hear. When she had told him that she loved him, Jace had responded by drawing her into his arms and kissing her until she'd trembled with desire. But she had just heard him say that she was unremarkable.

She stared at her reflection in the full-length mirror on the wall and the scales fell from her eyes. Her new dress that she'd rushed out and bought when Jace had invited her to spend the weekend with him was a romantic froth of pink tulle, but it wasn't glamorous. She had tied her long hair back with a matching pink ribbon. The dress's sweetheart neckline was more daring than her usual restrained style, and before coming to meet Jace she had lost her nerve and covered up with a cardigan.

Compared to the elegant Parisian women Eleanor had noticed shopping on the Champs-Elysées, and who had no doubt caught Jace's eye, she was neither sophisticated nor sexy. In truth, she had wondered why he was attracted to her. It turned out that he'd been lying to her all along. Nausea churned in the pit of Eleanor's stomach. She had taken extra care putting on her make-up, but now tears spilled from her eyes and two black tracks of mascara ran down her cheeks.

She recalled that a few weeks after her grandfather had suffered a fatal heart attack, a man had come to Francine's—the hotel in Oxford owned by Gilpin Leisure—and introduced himself as Takis Samaras, CEO of a Greek luxury hotel chain, Perseus. He had been very keen to buy the Pangalos, but she'd told him she had no intention of selling any of Gilpin Leisure's assets.

Now she knew that Jace wanted the hotel and he did not care about her. She was devastated to discover what he really thought of her and she wanted to run away and hide like a wounded animal, but she forced herself to remain where she stood when he spoke again.

'Marriage to Eleanor is the only way I can claim back the hotel that her grandfather took from my father. I have discovered that a clause in Kostas's will stipulates that the Pangalos must remain within the family's ownership.' Jace swore. 'The wily old fox must have gloated, believing he had prevented me from getting my hands on the hotel that by rights should be half mine. But I met his granddaughter and it was easy to make Eleanor fall in love with me.'

Jace pocketed his phone and strode across the balcony. He'd heard a faint sound from inside his suite and through the voile curtain he glimpsed a shadowy figure. There was the faint click of a door closing and when he stepped into the room there was no one there.

His frown cleared when he saw on the table a cake box with the name of a Greek bakery on the lid, and he guessed that one of the hotel's staff had delivered it to his suite. He opened the box and smiled, certain that Eleanor was responsible for ordering the selection of sweet treats: *baklava, loukoumades* and his particular favourite, *kataifi*—little pastries drenched in almond syrup.

Jace drank alcohol in moderation and he had never taken drugs, but he had confessed to Eleanor that he had a sweet tooth. It was typical of her to have remembered and arranged the thoughtful gift. He ran his hand over the stubble on his jaw and swore beneath his breath as he thought of his diffident fiancée.

Two months ago, Jace had decided on a whim to visit the Pangalos Beach Resort on Sithonia, a peninsular in the region of Halkidiki in northern Greece. It was the first time he had returned to the hotel since he was eleven years old, and he'd been swamped by bitter memories of how he and his parents had been forcibly evicted from the building by Kostas's security staff.

The Pangalos had been extensively refurbished, and inside it was almost unrecognisable. But when Jace had stepped into the lobby he'd pictured his mother and father standing arm in arm, waiting to greet guests. It was the personal touches that made families return year after year, Jace's father had insisted. Guests who stayed at the Pangorakis hotel, which had been its name back then, were made to feel as though they were part of a big, happy family.

But Kostas had been determined to attract a different class of clientele: the super-rich, who wanted five-star luxury and were prepared to pay for it. Arguments about the future direction of the hotel had led to a breakdown in the two men's friendship, and Kostas, backed by money from his wealthy English wife and aided by influential Greek friends, had seized control of the Pangorakis, later changing its name to the Pangalos.

Six months ago Kostas had died suddenly and, to everyone's surprise, he had left his granddaughter Eleanor in charge of Gilpin Leisure. The company owned an upmarket boutique hotel, Francine's, in Oxford, and the Pangalos Beach Resort in Greece. By all accounts, Eleanor's older brother, Mark Buchanan, had been furious at being overlooked by his grandfather. Eleanor had appointed him as General Manager of the Pangalos, but Jace had heard rumours that Mark was more interested in playing blackjack in the casino than managing the hotel.

When Jace had strolled across the pool terrace he'd taken scant notice of a young woman sitting on a sun lounger, her head bowed over a book. But he'd overheard a waiter who had brought her a drink saying, 'Will that be all, Miss Buchanan?'

The name had caught Jace's attention and he'd recognised Eleanor from a newspaper photo when her grandfather's death had been announced. Nondescript was his first opinion of her. Dark blonde hair pulled back from an unprepossessing face. Pale skin, turning pink on her shoulders from the sun. Good legs, he'd noted, before skimming his eyes over her shapely figure.

She was wearing a one-piece swimsuit that covered her body from neck to thigh but nevertheless did not disguise the gentle curves of her hips and the firm swell of her breasts. Oddly, Jace had found her modest costume more alluring than the skimpy bikinis worn by other women sunbathing by the pool. In his opinion, the unknown was intriguing, rather like a birthday present that was still wrapped.

There had been no plan in his head when he'd sat down on a vacant sun lounger next to Eleanor. He had flirted with women since he was a teenager and discovered that his dark good looks and muscular physique commanded female attention. With consummate skill he had drawn Eleanor into conversation. He'd watched her closely when he had introduced himself, but she had shown no reaction to his name.

To his surprise, Kostas's granddaughter was charming, if a little too serious. Eliciting one of her rare smiles became a challenge, and the upward curve of her wide mouth had an unexpected effect on Jace's libido. He had decided that it might be useful to get to know her better, but marriage had not been in his mind when he'd joined her on a cruise around the islands of Thasos and Lemnos.

During the trip, Eleanor had confided that she felt overwhelmed by the responsibility that had been thrust on her by her grandfather. 'I want to fulfil Pappoús's expectations, and I hope he would be proud of me,' she'd told Jace. 'He established the Pangalos hotel and made it a success without help from anyone.'

Jace had gritted his teeth at hearing how Kostas had rewritten the hotel's history without crediting the hard work and sacrifice his father had made. But it was clear that Eleanor had loved her grandfather, and Jace had held back from telling her the truth—that Kostas had ruthlessly conned Dimitri out of his share of the business that the two men had started together.

Jace had been fifteen when he'd found his father's body at the bottom of a cliff. Incredibly, Dimitri had still been alive and with his last breaths he had entreated Jace to take back the family's share of the hotel on Sithonia for his mother's sake. For twenty years Jace had been driven by his hatred of Kostas and his determination to honour his father's dying plea. Eleanor was his chance, he'd realised. Marriage to her would allow him to claim part-ownership of the Pangalos hotel, and there was the added satisfaction of knowing that Kostas would turn in his grave.

The plan was perfect and yet so simple,

Jace thought now as he walked over to the bar and poured a generous measure of single malt whisky into a glass. He checked his watch. Two minutes to seven. Eleanor would be here soon. In fact, he was surprised that she hadn't arrived early for their celebratory dinner. Her infatuation with him had made it easy for him to seduce her.

He frowned as he recalled the look of stunned joy in Eleanor's hazel eyes when he'd asked her to marry him. Obviously, he had not told her the real reason why he had asked her to be his wife. His ultimate goal was to seize absolute ownership of the Pangalos. Kostas had ruined his father, and so he would ruin Kostas's legacy. Marriage was the price he was prepared to pay to get his hands on the hotel.

Jace sipped his whisky and brooded that marriage was a fool's game. Several of his friends had been stung with expensive divorce settlements. He was thankful that Katerina had turned him down years ago. Hell, it had hurt at the time, and for a while he'd nursed a broken heart. But her rejection had emphasised the life lesson he'd learned from Kostas's betrayal of his father. Loyalty counted for nothing and money was everything. Except that in this instance, even though Jace was a self-made multi-millionaire, he was prevented from buying the Pangalos by a clause in Kostas's will.

So he would marry Eleanor Buchanan and it would be a sweet victory to finally avenge his father's destruction. The only pity was that Kostas would never know he had lost. As for his blushing bride, Jace's body tightened in anticipation of taking Eleanor to bed later tonight. He knew she wanted him. Her ardent response when he kissed her had been a pleasant surprise. Rather more surprising was his urgency to make love to her. He sensed that her reserved nature hid a sensuality which he was looking forward to awakening.

As Takis had pointed out, Eleanor was not in the league of the sexually confident women Jace usually chose for his lovers. He kept his life free from emotional entanglements and he planned to do the same when he married. When Eleanor was his wife he would provide her with a luxurious lifestyle for the duration of their marriage, and he would give her a generous divorce settlement. He dismissed a twinge of guilt that he was involving her in a feud which she was unaware of.

Deeply satisfied with the way things had worked out, he drank the rest of his whisky and checked his watch again. One of the things he liked about his fiancée was her punctuality. He had left nothing to chance, and had wooed Eleanor diligently for the past couple of months, flying over to England most weekends to see her. Every time he'd collected her to take her out to dinner she had been waiting on the doorstep and hadn't disguised her pleasure at seeing him. Thinking of Eleanor's eagerness evoked another pang of guilt as Jace acknowledged that he would never love her.

There was a knock on the door and Jace went to open it, wondering why Eleanor had not used the key card he'd given her.

'Monsieur Zagorakis.' The concierge stood in the corridor. 'I have a package for you from Mademoiselle Buchanan.'

'*Merci.*' Jace frowned as he took the sealed envelope from the man. He closed the door and ripped open the envelope. The diamond engagement ring that he had placed on Eleanor's finger earlier in the day fell into his palm. What the hell?

The accompanying note was brief.

I know what you did and I don't want to marry you.

Jace's jaw clenched. His mind flew back to when he had been a young man and he recalled Katerina's mocking rejection of his marriage proposal. He'd saved his wages from his job as a labourer on a building site for months so that he could buy her an engagement ring, but she had looked scathingly at the tiny diamond he'd proudly offered her.

'*Of course I'm not going to marry you! I want a husband with money and career prospects,*' Katerina told him. '*Not someone who spent time in prison and has a criminal record. You're a sexy stud, Jace, but you are not good enough for me.*'

Soon after, he'd heard that Katerina had married a wealthy shipping tycoon who was old enough to be her father. Jace reread Eleanor's note and something black and ugly coiled through him when he realised that she must have found out about his past.

He'd seen no reason to tell her. It had happened a long time ago and he'd paid his debt to society. The stakes had been too high. He hadn't explained that he'd been to prison, fearing she might refuse to marry him. No marriage meant no hotel, and no possibility of honouring the promise he had made to his father.

Jace stared at the diamond ring glittering in his palm and swore. He picked up the phone and pressed the number for Eleanor's room. She did not answer, and her mobile went straight to voicemail. Cursing, he put a call through to the reception desk and learned that Mademoiselle Buchanan had checked out five minutes ago.

Theos. Anger ran like molten lava through Jace's veins as his plan to reclaim the Pangalos unravelled. It had always been about the hotel, but there was an inexplicable heaviness in his chest when he thought of Eleanor. She had seemed besotted with him, yet she'd left without a word. Why hadn't she given him a chance to explain what had really happened when he'd been given a prison sentence?

The answer was obvious to him. Despite his wealth and his meteoric rise to success, he could not escape from his past. He had clawed his way out of the gutter, but Eleanor must have decided that he was not good enough to be her husband, Jace thought bitterly.

CHAPTER ONE

One year later

ELEANOR LOVED THE peace and tranquillity of flying in a hot-air balloon. The balloon floated on the breeze, creating a magical sensation of stillness and silence. She could taste the crisp morning air and feel the sun on her face.

After gaining her private pilot's licence six months ago, she and another pilot, Nigel, had clubbed together to buy a balloon and they took it in turns to fly whenever the weather was suitable. The conditions were perfect this morning. She had met Nigel and the ground crew in a field before dawn, and they had helped her to inflate the balloon and heat the air inside the canopy with the burner. Eleanor had climbed into the basket, the ropes were untied and the balloon rose gently into the sky.

The mist had cleared with the sunrise and the view over the Oxfordshire countryside from two thousand feet up was breathtaking. In the distance she could see the graceful spires of the university buildings, while below, the River Thames was a ribbon of silvery blue curling through the green fields. As the balloon drifted serenely over a park, she heard dogs barking and recognised the sweet song of a skylark.

Her first experience of ballooning had been as a child when she'd been diagnosed with scoliosis and had to wear a back brace to prevent the curve in her spine from getting worse. She had hated being trapped in a rigid plastic jacket that fitted underneath her arms and went down to her hips. Her condition had prevented her from doing many physical activities, but her parents had continued to take her brother and sister on adventure holidays and skiing trips. Eleanor had stayed with her grandparents and she'd put on a brave face and assured everyone that she did not mind missing out on family events. But inside she'd felt hurt. Scoliosis made her different, a problem for her parents, and, she was convinced, less loveable than Mark and Lissa.

Her grandfather had been the only person who'd seemed to understand how Eleanor felt. One time when her parents and siblings were away, Pappoús had arranged for her to have a flight in a hot-air balloon. It had been an amazing experience and while in the air she had forgotten about her back pain and lack of mobility.

Since her surgery she had been able to lead a normal life, but she'd continued to suffer from a lack of self-confidence. Hearing Jace describe her as unremarkable had spurred Eleanor on to prove to herself that he was wrong, and she had fulfilled her dream of becoming a balloon pilot.

Flying required her to stay focused and in the moment, and today more than ever she was glad of the distraction to stop herself from remembering that a year ago Jace had proposed to her. *No*, she would not think about him, she ordered herself. And she definitely wouldn't cry. She'd wasted enough tears on Jace Zagorakis.

Down on the ground, something glittered

brightly and caught her attention. It was probably caused by the sun on a window, but the sparkle evoked memories of the diamond engagement ring Jace had placed on her finger. Eleanor screwed up her eyes to hold back her tears that brimmed despite her best effort to banish them, along with memories of the lying Greek who had shattered her heart. She had not told anyone about her engagement, which was probably the shortest on record, she thought bitterly.

She'd had a lucky escape, she reminded herself. If she hadn't overheard Jace's phone conversation she would have slept with him in Paris. And she would have married him, unaware that he did not love her. All he'd wanted was the hotel on Sithonia. Eleanor brushed away a tear. A year ago she'd listened to her heart and ignored her common sense, which had warned that sexy, charismatic Jace was out of her league.

She forced her mind from the past, frustrated that she had allowed memories of Jace to infiltrate her aerial sanctuary. Flying the balloon gave her a sense of identity and pride that she had completed the extensive training and passed the exams to earn her pilot's licence. After an hour she looked for a suitable field where she could land and contacted the ground crew on the two-way radio to tell them where to meet her. Bringing the balloon down required all her piloting skills as she controlled the rate of descent. When she was safely down on the ground and the balloon had been packed away, she congratulated herself for not thinking about Jace for a whole hour.

Balloons could only fly early in the morning or in the evening when the air was cooler and more stable. By ten a.m. Eleanor was driving through the centre of Oxford on her way back to Francine's. The hotel had been named after her English grandmother, whose family had bought the historic property and turned it into the finest hotel in the county.

For the past year Eleanor had thrown herself into work. Before her grandfather had died, he'd talked about updating the Oxford hotel's rather dated interior. When Eleanor had inherited the company, she'd pushed ahead with plans for Francine's to undergo an extensive refurbishment. It had meant closing the hotel for three months while the work was carried out, and the loss of revenue, combined with escalating building costs had led to a dramatic dip in Gilpin Leisure's profits.

Fortunately, the Pangalos was doing well, so her brother had assured her. She had put Mark in charge of the beach resort to make up for him being snubbed by their grandfather. Since she'd broken off her engagement, she had distanced herself from the place where she'd first met Jace. There was no reason why she would have to meet the lying toad ever again, but to be on the safe side Eleanor did not plan on going to Greece any time soon.

An expensive-looking black saloon car was parked at the front of Francine's when Eleanor drove onto the forecourt. Business had been slow to pick up since the hotel had reopened, but the marketing department had run a promotional campaign to attract new bookings. With any luck, whoever owned the luxury car would decide to stay in the most expensive suite for a month, she thought as she drove round to the back of the hotel.

A private wing adjoining the main building had been Eleanor's home since her parents had died in an accident when she was twelve, and she and her brother and sister had been brought up by their grandparents. She had a meeting with the hotel's event's manager scheduled for eleven o'clock and ran up to her room to change her clothes before heading into the kitchen to grab a coffee.

She was surprised to find that her sister was up and dressed before midday. Lissa lived in London and only came back to Oxford occasionally, usually when she wanted money. Pappoús's decision to put Eleanor in control of her sister's trust fund until Lissa was twenty-five had put a further strain on their relationship.

'Where have you been?' Lissa yawned and sounded uninterested. She did not wait for Eleanor to reply. 'There's a guy here to see you. He didn't give his name, but he said that he's involved with a hotel chain in Greece called Poseidon...or Perseus. Something like that.'

Eleanor's heart had stopped when Lissa mentioned Greece. 'I've heard of Perseus Hotels,' she said flatly. Fifteen months ago Takis Samaras had been very keen to buy the Pangalos, but now she knew that he had been sent by Jace. 'Did Mary give any more details about this man?' She was surprised that her secretary hadn't asked the visitor to make an appointment.

Lissa shook her head and her platinum blonde bob swirled around her face. 'He didn't go into the hotel. He came to the house.' She grimaced. 'The doorbell woke me up. He insisted that he has something important to discuss with you and he's waiting in the sitting room.'

Eleanor shrugged. 'I have an idea what he wants, but he's wasting his time. It was Pappoús's wish that the Pangalos remains in the family's ownership.'

'And of course you would never go against his wishes,' Lissa mocked. 'Even when we were children you were always boringly well-behaved. I guess that's why Pappoús made you his heir.'

'I take my responsibility for Gilpin Leisure seriously, but it doesn't mean that I'm boring,' Eleanor muttered, stung by her sister's comment.

Lissa's brows rose. 'You dress like a nun,

you hardly ever go out, and you haven't had a serious relationship in living memory.'

Eleanor bit her lip. For the brief time she'd been dating Jace, her sister had been in California, trying to launch an acting career. Lissa's dig about her clothes was unfair. She glanced down at her black pencil skirt, white blouse and black cardigan, teamed with low-heeled black court shoes. 'I have to dress smartly for work,' she defended herself.

'Take my advice and ditch the cardigan,' Lissa told her. 'The Greek guy is a hunk and he's not likely to take an interest in you when you're dressed like his mother.'

'I don't want him to take an interest in me.' God forbid, Eleanor thought with a shudder. One devious Greek was enough. Jace had broken her heart and she would never be idiotic enough to trust a man ever again.

She finished her coffee and walked down the hallway, but hesitated outside the sitting room. A year ago she had felt utterly humiliated when she'd overheard Jace state the real reason he had asked her to marry him. If he had sent his friend to Oxford for a second time to try to persuade her to sell the Pangalos, she would let Takis know that he'd had a wasted journey.

Eleanor opened the sitting room door and her eyes flew to the tall, imposing figure standing facing the window, silhouetted against the brightness outside. He had haunted her dreams too often, and she instantly recognised the breadth of his shoulders and the arrogant tilt of his head.

'*You?*' Her breath was squeezed out of her lungs and she clung to the door handle as her legs turned to jelly.

Jace Zagorakis turned around and Eleanor's heart stopped beating as she stared at his chiselled features that were imprinted on her psyche. He was still sinfully beautiful, but his face seemed harder, the high cheekbones sharper, giving him a predatory look that made her heart slam against her ribcage.

From across the room his eyes appeared to be black, but she knew that they were the colour of bittersweet chocolate and fringed by impossibly long black lashes. His thick, dark brown hair was stylishly groomed but curled rebelliously over his collar, and his facial stubble did not disguise the uncompromising set of his square jaw.

Eleanor's gaze was drawn to his mouth that curved in a sardonic smile as if he were amused by her startled reaction to him. What had he expected? she wondered. Had he thought that she would be pleased to see him?

For months after she'd fled from his hotel suite in Paris, she had hoped he would come after her and explain that it had all been a misunderstanding, and he was really in love with her. But he hadn't contacted her in a year and her misery had turned to anger and disillusionment. She was tempted to run away from the man who had treated her with such callous disregard. But Eleanor Buchanan was not a coward and she uncurled her fingers from the door handle and lifted her chin as she walked further into the room.

'This is a surprise, Jace. Although I can't say it's a pleasant one.' She was pleased that she sounded composed even though her heart was thumping.

He strolled towards her, but to her relief he halted several feet away. An amused smile still played on his lips, but his eyes resting on her face were watchful.

'I recall a time when you were pleased to see me, Eleanor,' he drawled. His gravelly voice with its discernible Greek accent was deliciously sexy and Eleanor could not control a quiver of response to his raw masculinity.

She flushed, remembering that when they had been dating and Jace had come to Oxford to visit her, she had run into his arms, eager for his kiss. She had been like an exuberant puppy wagging its tail for its master's attention, she thought with embarrassment.

'Why are you here?' she demanded.

His brows rose at her abrupt tone. 'I want to talk to you.'

'I'm busy. If you have something important to discuss, I suggest you speak to my secretary to arrange an appointment.' She glared at him, her anger mounting. How dare he walk back into her life as if nothing had happened? 'You lost the right to want anything from me after what you did.'

Jace's dark eyes flashed, but Eleanor sensed

the effort he made to control his temper. 'What did I do?' he asked mildly.

'Don't pretend you don't know. I *heard* you.' Her voice shook with emotions she was desperate to hide from him. 'I came to your hotel room in Paris and overheard you talking on your phone to Takis Samaras. You told him that you planned to marry me because you wanted my grandfather's hotel.'

'So it was you who left a box of pastries,' Jace murmured. His eyes searched her face intently, as if he were trying to read her thoughts. 'And you listened in on my private conversation. Was that the reason you ran out on me without telling me you were leaving? You switched off your phone and I had no way of knowing if you were safe.'

'Like you cared,' she mocked. 'Of course it's why I left. Do you think I would have stayed and pretended that everything was all right between us after I'd discovered that you didn't…that you don't…?' She broke off and bit down hard on her lip so that she tasted blood.

'I don't what?' he prompted.

Eleanor closed her eyes and when she opened

them again he was still there in front of her, not a figment of her imagination but a living, breathing, impossibly handsome man who had never given a damn about her.

'You don't love me,' she said flatly. 'Do you?'

His silence extinguished the tiny flame of hope that had burned valiantly inside her. What a fool she was to have wondered if his visit was because he had realised that he had feelings for her after all. Bitterness filled the void where her heart had been until Jace had ripped it out.

'I don't suppose it was a coincidence that you went to the Pangalos last spring,' she said dully. 'You must have known I was staying there, and you made a point of introducing yourself. But you only pretended to be interested in me.'

He frowned. 'That's not true. I went to the hotel by chance and recognised you.'

'I told you I was leaving the next day for a cruise around the islands. Was it a coincidence that you joined the yacht just before it was about to sail? I don't think so,' she answered for him. 'I think you deliberately set out to seduce me, and you plotted to seize control of the Pangalos because of an alleged feud between your father and my grandfather.'

'The feud was real,' Jace said harshly. 'My father and Kostas were best friends until your grandfather got greedy. He and his clever lawyers conned my father out of his half-share of the hotel. But it wasn't only that my father was bankrupt and he and my mother lost everything they had worked for, including our home.' Jace's jaw hardened. 'My father was devastated that his friend, who he had trusted and loved, showed him no loyalty. Kostas destroyed my father and broke his heart.'

'And so you decided to break mine. Is that why you did it?' Eleanor's voice cracked. 'You wanted revenge for a crime that frankly I don't even believe happened. My grandfather was a good man and he would not have behaved in a way that was illegal or immoral. But what *you* did was unforgivable.'

She dashed her hand over her face and was mortified to find her cheeks were wet. 'I was a sexual innocent and I didn't stand a chance against you—an experienced playboy.'

The air between them crackled with tension. Eleanor wondered when Jace had stepped nearer to her without her being aware of him moving. He loomed over her, six-feet-plus of physical perfection and so close that her senses were assailed by the spicy scent of his aftershave.

'Are you saying you were a virgin when we met?' he asked curtly. 'You spoke in the past tense, so does that mean you are no longer one?'

She clenched her hands by her sides and fought the temptation to slap his arrogantly beautiful face. 'It's none of your damned business.'

Jace did not know why he had probed Eleanor about her private life. Even more inexplicable was the surge of jealousy he felt at the idea of her in another man's bed. It wasn't as if they had been lovers and, even if they had, he'd never had a problem moving on at the end of a relationship. Admittedly, he hadn't wanted their engagement to be over, but that was only because he had needed to marry Eleanor to acquire the Pangalos hotel.

Jace could have sworn that he did not have a possessive bone in his body, but he felt an overwhelming urge to pull Eleanor into his arms and kiss the sulky line of her mouth until her lips softened beneath his. A year ago he had enjoyed her eager response to his caresses more than he'd cared to admit. When she'd walked into the room a few minutes ago, his heart had banged against his ribs.

He remembered on the yacht in Greece she had worn a one-piece swimsuit that moulded her gorgeous curves. From the start he had been attracted to Eleanor's understated sensuality and his fingers itched to unbutton her prim blouse and cradle her full breasts in his hands. Chemistry still existed between them, simmering beneath the surface. Desire heated Jace's blood and his body tightened. He hadn't felt this alive for the past year, and he was confident that if he kissed Eleanor her resistance would melt.

'You must have laughed at me behind my back,' she said with a catch in her voice. 'I fell in love with you, but it was all just a game to you, wasn't it?'

He did not know how to answer her, and

guilt was an uncomfortable weight in the pit of his stomach. He wished he could wipe away the tear that slid down her cheek, but he knew he'd lost the right to comfort her after he'd callously used her. Eleanor had simply been a means to an end. He had seen an opportunity to reclaim the hotel that his father had been cheated out of by her grandfather and he'd seized it without considering the impact his behaviour might have on her.

In his mind, Jace saw his father's battered and bloodied body. Dimitri had died from his injuries without revealing if he had walked too close to the edge of the cliff and fallen by accident, or if he'd jumped. The inquest had been inconclusive, but if Dimitri had chosen to end his life then Kostas Pangalos had blood on his hands, Jace thought grimly.

'It was never a game,' he told Eleanor. 'It was about reclaiming my father's share of the Pangalos and you were collateral damage.'

She inhaled sharply. 'God, you bastard.'

His jaw clenched. 'Believe what you like, but if you had married me I would have endeavoured to be a good husband. I hated your grandfather, but I would have treated you well.'

'*Treated me well?*' Her hazel eyes turned almost green when she was angry, Jace noticed. 'I'm not a puppy you could train to sit up and beg for scraps of your attention.'

'I never thought of you in that way. I liked that you did not hold anything back in your response to me.' His eyes narrowed on the betraying pink stain that spread over her face. 'And I think you still want me.' He could read the signs. Her pupils were huge, dark orbs and she was breathing fast so that her breasts rose and fell jerkily. 'If I kissed you now, would you push me away?'

She recoiled as if he were the devil. 'I hate you. The thought of your touch revolts me.'

'*Theos!*' Jace raked his hand through his hair when Eleanor spun away from him and retreated to stand behind the sofa. He did not know why he had challenged her, or why he had wanted to provoke her into admitting that desire was still a potent force between them.

'I'd like you to leave,' she said stiffly. 'Whatever you came here for, I'm not interested.'

'I guarantee you will be after you've heard

what I'm about to tell you concerning the Pangalos.' He walked across the room and lowered himself into an armchair.

'You're wasting your time. A stipulation in my grandfather's will prevents me from selling the hotel.' Eleanor's eyes flashed. 'Even if it were possible, I wouldn't sell it to you if my life depended on it.'

'I wonder what you would be prepared to do to keep your brother out of prison.'

'I don't know what you are up to, Jace. But I won't fall for your lies again.'

His jaw tightened. He hadn't expected Eleanor to welcome him with open arms, but her contemptuous tone riled him. 'I never lied to you.'

'You let me think that you were in love with me.'

'Did I actually say so?'

She stared at him and he sensed the effort it took her to control her emotions. 'No,' she muttered at last. 'I thought you were a prince. But I discovered that you are just a man, and not a nice one.'

'What you felt was infatuation based on sexual attraction,' he growled, trying to ignore the tug of remorse he felt when she brushed her hand across her eyes. 'If you had married me, the Pangalos hotel would not be in its current dire financial situation.'

Eleanor shook her head. 'I don't believe you. If there was a problem my brother would have told me.'

'Your brother *is* the problem.' Jace's patience evaporated. 'Sit down, Eleanor, and listen to me. The Pangalos has huge debts and could be forced into insolvency.'

He had her attention now. She walked around the sofa and sat down on the end furthest away from him. 'You're lying. I spoke to Mark a few days ago and he told me that the hotel is fully booked for the rest of the summer.'

'Most of the bookings are package deals bought through holiday companies, but you know as well as I do that the hotel won't receive money for the rooms it lets out for several months. In the meantime the staff need to be paid and there are the running costs of the hotel. There is also an outstanding tax bill owed to the Greek government that your brother failed to pay. If the Pangalos is forced to declare bankruptcy, then you, as the director of Gilpin Leisure, will be legally required to close down the hotel and sell off its assets to pay back the creditors.'

Eleanor had paled while Jace spoke. She leapt to her feet. 'What you have told me is a pack of lies. You can't possibly know confidential financial details about the Pangalos.'

'It would appear that I know more than you,' Jace said drily. 'I have a reliable source of information and I understand that when you inherited Gilpin Leisure you gave control of the Pangalos to your brother.'

'Mark was devastated that my grandfather made me his successor. My brother is the oldest grandchild and it was assumed that he would inherit the company.' She sighed. 'I don't know why Pappoús chose me. His decision caused a lot of resentment from my brother and sister towards me.'

'Kostas wouldn't have cared about that. He was first and foremost a ruthless businessman, and it's my guess that he put you at the head of the company because you are more sensible than either of your siblings.'

'By sensible I suppose you mean boring.'

'I did not find you boring during our relationship, *pouláki mou.*' His body stirred as he remembered the softness of her lips when he'd kissed her and how she had opened her mouth to the gentle pressure of his to allow his tongue access to her moist interior.

'You likened me to a drab sparrow,' she said flatly. 'We didn't have a relationship, but you fooled me into thinking that we did.'

Jace stood up and studied Eleanor's shuttered expression. The woman he'd met fifteen months ago had been shy with him at first, but she had gradually opened up. There was a vulnerability about her now that smote his conscience. He had not intentionally set out to hurt her, and he regretted that it had happened. But he would not be swayed from his determination to take back the Pangalos hotel.

'I suggest you contact your brother and ask him to explain the state of affairs. The only way you can save the Pangalos is if you find someone who will be willing to put money into the business. But it won't be easy to persuade an investor to take on the hotel's enormous debts. That's why you need me. I am prepared to rescue the Pangalos in return for you giving me fifty per cent ownership of the hotel.'

Eleanor's eyes flashed with anger. 'You must be joking. I wouldn't give you the time of day. Even if there is some truth in what you have told me, which I seriously doubt, I won't allow your grubby hands anywhere near the hotel that meant so much to my grandfather.'

Jace controlled his temper with difficulty. 'All I am asking is that you give back what should be mine. Your grandfather stole my father's share of the Pangalos, and it is only fair that you should return it to me.'

'Life isn't fair. If it was, I wouldn't have met you,' Eleanor said coldly.

Her jibe stung. 'You don't mean that,' Jace murmured. He watched Eleanor's eyes widen when he stepped closer to her. The pulse at the base of her throat was beating erratically. 'You can tell yourself that you hate me, but a year ago the passion was real for both of us.'

He wanted to kiss her one more time and taste her sweet breath in his mouth. When he lowered his face towards hers, he heard her catch her breath. For a split second Jace was tempted to forget about the feud between their families, which had nothing to do with him and Eleanor.

An image flashed into his mind of his father's body sprawled at the bottom of the cliff. His sanity returned and he jerked his mouth away from the temptation of Eleanor's lips.

'Pappoús entrusted the Pangalos to me and I will never share it with you,' she said tautly.

'Never say never,' Jace drawled. Eleanor would discover that she needed his help. But he had waited more than twenty years to avenge his father's death, and he could wait a little longer. He took a business card from his wallet and held it out to her. She did not take it and he dropped it down on the coffee table. 'When you call me and beg for my help, you had better hope that I will treat you more fairly than Kostas treated my father.'

CHAPTER TWO

'MARK! THANK GOD!' Relief poured through Eleanor when her brother answered his phone. 'Where are you? I've been so worried. You disappeared two days ago, and your phone was switched off.' She took a deep breath. 'I'm at the Pangalos. The auditors have found discrepancies with the accounts.'

'I know where you are. Lissa warned me that you left Oxford in a hurry to go to Greece. The truth is that I couldn't face you, El.'

'You spoke to Lissa but not to me?' Eleanor tried to ignore a stab of jealousy that her brother and sister shared a bond which she was excluded from. It had been the same when they were growing up. She had been the awkward middle child—not bold and daring like Mark, and lacking Lissa's precocious prettiness. Her scoliosis had set her further apart from her siblings and glamorous parents, and she had become more introverted and found solace in books.

'I don't understand what has been happening.' She had felt guilty for sending the auditors to check over the Pangalos's accounts after Jace had accused her brother of financial irregularities. Mark would be able to explain why money was missing, she assured herself. 'It has been discovered that you transferred money out of the Pangalos's account into your private bank account. The hotel owes money to many of its suppliers. There is an unpaid final tax demand and the staff haven't been paid their salaries this month.'

'It's a mess, I know,' her brother groaned. 'I only needed one big win and I could have replaced all the money.'

Eleanor's heart plummeted. 'You promised that you had stopped gambling. I put you in charge of the Pangalos because you gave me an assurance that you had sorted your life out and were ready to take on the responsibility of managing the hotel.'

'I swear I tried to give up. But the adrenalin rush is like a drug. I placed a few bets online and to start with I won back all I'd gambled and more. But then my losses started to mount up and I borrowed money from the hotel, intending to pay it back with my next big win.'

'But, surprise, surprise, you didn't win.' Eleanor bit her lip. She knew that gambling could be an addiction as serious as alcoholism or drugs. Her brother needed help, not criticism. 'Why didn't you tell me?'

'I was sure my luck would change. I didn't want to admit that I had mucked up again,' Mark said in a low voice. 'Grandfather was right when he made you his successor instead of me. I thought I had got lucky a few months ago when I was introduced to a Greek entrepreneur at a party. I'd had a fair bit to drink, to be honest, and when I mentioned that I had a cash flow problem, Jace was really understanding.'

'Jace?' Eleanor said sharply.

'Jace Zagorakis. He owns a property development company, Zagorakis Estates, and has a stake in a luxury hotel chain called Perseus. He's a well-known figure in Greece. Have you heard of him?'

'Vaguely,' Eleanor said through gritted teeth.

'Well, he offered to lend me money so that I could replace what I'd taken from the Pangalos.' Mark spoke quickly, stumbling over his words. 'But I didn't replace it. I gambled with it because the odds were in my favour. I was due a big win. It was my turn and I was certain I would hit the jackpot.'

'How much did you lose?' Eleanor felt sick when her brother told her. 'So there is no money to pay the Pangalos's bills.'

'It's worse than that. Zagorakis has demanded full repayment of the money I owe him, and he's threatened to take me to court if I don't pay up. As a named director of the Pangalos, I can be held personally liable for its debts. The hotel could be forced into insolvency and there is a good chance I would be sent to prison for tax evasion.'

Mark fell silent again and when he next spoke Eleanor was chilled by the darkness in his voice. 'I'll be honest, El. I've seriously thought about ending it all so that I can be with Mum and Dad.'

She inhaled sharply. 'Don't say that.'

'I still miss them.'

'I know,' she said gently. 'I miss them too.'

When her parents had died, Lissa, the baby of the family, had received the most attention from other relatives while Eleanor had retreated further inside herself. Grief had made Mark an angry and difficult teenager. But at night Eleanor had often heard him crying in his bedroom. She had wanted to go in and comfort him, but she'd felt unsure that he would welcome her, and she'd crept back to her own room.

'I'll find a way to sort out the problems at the Pangalos,' she told her brother. How, she did not know, but she was desperate to reassure him. 'Mark, please look after yourself. Where are you?'

'Ireland. It was the last holiday we had with Mum and Dad. Do you remember we stayed at a riding stables and took the horses out every day?'

'I didn't go with you. It was before my back surgery and I couldn't ride because I had to wear the body brace.'

Eleanor had overheard her parents discussing the difficulties of taking her on a horse-riding holiday because of her spinal condition. Their relief when she had offered to stay with her grandparents had been obvious, and she had tried not to feel hurt. After the holiday, her brother and sister had returned to England and her parents had flown to Sri Lanka, where they had died in an accident without her ever seeing them again.

Scoliosis had affected her childhood and her relationship with her family, she acknowledged sadly. But now Mark needed her help and she would do everything she possibly could to save him and the Pangalos hotel.

Eleanor ended the call after eliciting a promise from her brother that he would seek professional help for his problems. With mounting despair she studied the columns of figures in front of her, which added up to the staggering debt that Mark had accrued. Ordinarily, she would have been able to transfer money between Francine's and the Pangalos to cover the unpaid bills, but the Oxford hotel had not made a profit for three months while it was being refurbished. Eleanor had taken out a business loan to pay for the work, and her application to the bank for more credit had been turned down.

Fortunately, Gilpin Leisure had reserves

which she could use to pay the staff's wages and cover most of the Pangalos's running costs. But there was still the huge tax bill that Mark had omitted to pay, as well as the six-figure debt he owed to Jace Zagorakis.

Damn the man! Eleanor did not believe it had been a coincidence that Jace had met her brother at a party. He had used his charisma to gain Mark's trust, like he had gained hers. But Jace's ulterior motive was to take ownership of the Pangalos, which he insisted her grandfather had stolen from his father. When she had taken a look through the hotel's records, she had not found any evidence to confirm Jace's story. Dimitri Zagorakis had sold his share of the hotel to Kostas and the transaction had been overseen by lawyers.

She tried to quell a rising sense of panic as she faced the seriousness of the situation. It was stuffy in Mark's office, where she had been holed up for much of the past two days. She needed air, and she stood up and walked over to open the window. The office was on the top floor of the hotel and overlooked the resort's exclusive bungalows and the private beach that was one of the best on Sithonia. A long stretch of white sand ran down to a turquoise sea that was ideal for swimming, although most of the affluent guests preferred to sit on sun loungers, sipping cocktails.

Pappoús had been proud of the five-star holiday complex he had created but, unless Eleanor could find a solution to the Pangalos's financial crisis, she would be unable to save the hotel from bankruptcy. Guiltily, she accepted that she should have kept a closer eye on her brother. She'd put her faith in Mark and made him a director of the hotel because she had wanted her brother to like her, Eleanor acknowledged with painful honesty.

She walked back to the desk and her gaze fell on Jace's business card. He had been arrogantly confident that she would call him. Fury bubbled up inside her, but she could see no other option than to plead with him for more time to try to raise the money Mark owed him.

Her heart was thumping when she called the number on the card. A woman's voice spoke and said that she was Jace's PA. Jace was unlikely to have answered his office phone, Eleanor silently berated herself, feeling foolish because her mouth had dried at the prospect of speaking to him.

The PA listened to her request for a meeting with Jace before putting her on hold while she checked his diary. 'Mr Zagorakis can fit you in tomorrow at five p.m., Miss Buchanan,' she said when she came back on the line. 'He says he has been expecting to hear from you.'

Eleanor pictured a self-satisfied smirk on Jace's diabolically handsome face, and her temper sizzled. Feeling too restless to remain in the office, she took the lift down to the ground floor and walked through the magnificent marble-tiled lobby. When she'd visited the Pangalos as a child, she had thought it was a palace. Her grandfather had entrusted his beloved hotel to her, but she had allowed herself to be ruled by her emotions when she'd put her brother in charge.

As she walked past the hotel's boutique, she caught sight of herself in the glass shopfront and her steps slowed. Was the drab-looking woman with her hair scraped off her face really her? Her skirt was unfashionably long, and her cardigan that she'd pulled around her shoulders because the air-conditioning was chilly added years to her. Lissa had criticised her clothes for being frumpy. Far worse had been when she'd overheard Jace's opinion of her.

Unremarkable.

It still hurt, and tears pricked her eyes. But as Eleanor stared at her reflection she acknowledged that Jace had been right. She was old before her time and weighed down with the responsibility of running Gilpin Leisure. Long hours in the office back in Oxford meant that she never had time to shop for clothes or visit a hair salon, and her social life was non-existent.

Seeing Jace again had reinforced how jaw-droppingly handsome he was. How could she have believed that he had been attracted to *her* a year ago? Her beautiful sister was much more Jace's type. Eleanor bit her lip. During her childhood, she'd often felt lonely. When she'd met Jace it had felt like a fairy tale and she'd been flattered by his attention.

The truth was that she'd been desperate to be loved. But he hadn't loved her. He had made a fool of her and now she hated him. *Hated him!* But Jace was pulling all the strings and tomorrow she would have to throw herself on his mercy.

Pride stiffened Eleanor's backbone as much as the metal rods supporting her spine. She turned her gaze from her reflection in the shop window to the mannequin displaying a figure-hugging scarlet dress. Jace had likened her to a timid sparrow, but tomorrow he was going to get the shock of his life when he discovered that she would not give up a share of the Pangalos without a fight. And before she went into battle, Eleanor decided, stepping into the boutique, she needed some armour.

'Do you remember the parties in the ballroom, Jace?'

'I do.' Jace smiled at his mother. 'Every week you and Bampás hosted a party for the guests who were about to return home at the end of their holiday.'

The food and drink had been provided free of charge by his parents. It was a way of thanking the guests for choosing to stay at the Pangorakis hotel and to encourage them to return the following year, his father had said.

'The children had so much fun. I used to

love seeing their happy faces.' Iliana sighed softly. 'They were good times, before we lost the hotel. Your poor father never came to terms with what happened.' Her voice faded and she closed her eyes, the lashes making dark fans against her sallow skin. 'I wish...'

Jace leaned closer to the daybed in the orangery at his house in Thessaloniki where his mother spent much of her time these days. 'What do you wish, Mamá?'

'To go back just once more before... I leave this world.'

'The specialist thinks you could live for a year or more. He is confident the drugs will slow the spread of the cancer.'

Jace's throat felt constricted and he swallowed hard. He picked up his mother's hand and raised it to his lips to kiss her bony fingers. Her hands had scrubbed floors and done all sorts of menial work so that she could earn money to feed them both after his father had died.

Hatred of Kostas Pangalos festered like poison inside him. But he was close now to avenging his father and reclaiming the hotel. When he remembered how greatly his mother had suffered in the years since his father's death, Jace assured himself that his ultimate goal to seize complete control of the Pangalos so that it would no longer be Kostas's legacy was justified.

'Very soon I will take you back to the Pangalos and we will rename it the Zagorakis. Will that make you happy, Mamá?'

'How can you do that? Kostas...'

'Is dead. Today I intend to secure a deal which will see the hotel returned to us.'

Jace frowned when he thought of Eleanor. He had backed her into a corner, and he knew she had no choice but to give him a fifty per cent share of the Pangalos to save her brother's neck. She would only have turned to him as a last resort, which meant she had failed to raise enough money to pay off Mark Buchanan's debts.

Taking back the hotel had been his driving force for the whole of his adult life, but Jace did not feel as satisfied as he'd expected. Eleanor had made it clear that she despised him. When he'd asked her to marry him a year ago, he had deliberately not spoken of love. But guilt tugged uncomfortably in his gut when he remembered how unworldly Eleanor had been. She had made an unexpected impression on him and he'd found himself thinking about her often since she had broken off their engagement.

He forced his mind away from the memory of Eleanor's tears when he'd sprung a visit on her in England a week ago, and realised that his mother was speaking.

'You are a good son, Jace. When you were sent to prison I cried every night because I could not afford lawyers to fight your case. It was a travesty of justice.'

Jace's jaw clenched. Prison had been hell, and he still felt bitter that he'd been found guilty of a crime because of a rich man's lies. There were parallels between what had happened to him and how Kostas had employed corrupt lawyers to seize control of the Pangalos from his father. A few years ago, Jace had bought out the company owned by the man who had been responsible for him going to prison and immediately fired him. Now he was poised to reclaim the Pangalos, but in another twist of fate his mother was terminally ill.

'I take my own justice,' he murmured. There was steel beneath his soft voice. 'My business interests have made me very wealthy and you do not have to worry about me, Mamá.'

'I do worry about you though. When I am gone, you will be alone. I wish I could live long enough to see you married and settled with a woman who you love as much as your father and I loved each other.'

'None of us knows what the future holds,' Jace said diplomatically. There was no point upsetting his mother by telling her there was zero chance of him marrying for romantic reasons. He had believed he was in love once, but Katerina had proved that real love, the selfless, unconditional kind that his parents had shared, was a rarity.

An odd thought came into his mind. If his engagement to Eleanor has lasted for longer than a day, he was certain his mother would have liked her and approved of her as his future wife. But he could not turn the clock back.

Before he left for his office he had a quiet word with Anna, his mother's nurse. 'Try to persuade her to eat something. She needs to build up her strength.'

'I'll do my best,' the nurse promised, 'but she has a poor appetite.'

The day dragged. Jace told himself that the hours passed slowly because he was impatient to finalise the deal to reclaim the Pangalos that had been his goal since he was fifteen. It definitely had nothing to do with the prospect of seeing Eleanor again. His edgy mood was exacerbated by the oppressive atmosphere. A storm had been forecast, and outside his office window sullen grey clouds were mustering in the sky.

Just before five o'clock, the nurse phoned his private mobile number and explained that his mother had tripped over in the garden. 'She is not injured other than some bruising, but she is upset and would like to speak to you,' the nurse said.

While Jace was talking to his mother, his PA put her head round the door and informed him that Miss Buchanan had arrived. He glanced at his watch and noted that Eleanor was as punctual as ever. 'Tell her that I will see her shortly,' he mouthed to Rena.

His mother was sobbing on the phone. 'I am a silly old woman, and a burden to you.'

'Of course you are not a burden.'

'I won't be for much longer,' his mother choked. 'We both know the truth, Jace. I am dying. It breaks my heart that I'll never meet the woman you eventually marry. If I could only be sure that you will be in a happy relationship it would not hurt so much to leave you.'

Consoling his mother took some time and when he finally said goodbye to her Jace sighed heavily. It occurred to him that if his original plan to marry Eleanor a year ago had happened, his mother would have had peace of mind in her last months. It was a shame he couldn't change things. Before Eleanor had discovered the truth behind his marriage proposal, she had been eager to be his wife. But what if he *could* turn the clock back to a year ago?

He pulled his mind from his thoughts when he noticed the time and realised that over half an hour had passed since Eleanor had arrived for their appointment. He stepped out of his office and met his PA in the corridor.

'Miss Buchanan left a few minutes ago. I explained that you were unavoidably detained, but she said that she refused to play mind games,' Rena said, giving him a puzzled look.

Cursing beneath his breath, Jace took the lift down to the ground floor. He was incensed that Eleanor had walked out on him *again*! He'd been gutted when she had left him in Paris. Her abrupt departure then had stirred memories of the sense of abandonment he'd felt after his father had died, leaving the unanswered question of whether Dimitri had chosen to end his life. Jace had learned valuable lessons in the past. Good things never lasted, the people you cared about left and happiness was ephemeral.

His heart sank when he strode through the lobby, which was empty apart from the receptionist sitting behind a desk. Eleanor had gone. *Theos*, he had banked on her needing his help. Did she have a rich lover who she had persuaded to pay off her brother's debts? Why the hell did the idea of her in another man's arms make his blood boil?

Ahead of him, a woman emerged from

the cloakroom and walked quickly towards the revolving glass doors. Her stiletto heels clipped against the marble floor. Jace's eyes travelled up her shapely legs to the hem of her short red dress that stopped several inches above her knees. Her dark blonde hair had streaks of paler gold and fell in sexy layers to just below her shoulders. Something about the sway of her hips as she walked seemed familiar. But it couldn't be…

She was almost at the exit. '*Wait.*' Jace increased his pace and caught up with her. He put his hand on her arm and felt her stiffen when he spun her round to face him. '*Eleanor?*' He stared at her, stunned by her transformation from the demure woman who had briefly been his fiancée to this dangerously beautiful, scarlet-clad siren.

'You have no right to manhandle me,' she snapped. Her hazel eyes turned green and flashed with fury.

Jace dropped his hand down to his side, but his body refused to obey his brain and move away from her. His nostrils flared as he breathed in her perfume—a sultry, sensual fragrance that sent a rush of heat to his groin.

A year ago he had been attracted to Eleanor's understated prettiness, but this new and exciting version of the woman he had once planned to marry was intriguing and *hot*!

His jaw hardened when he saw her glance towards the door. Jace knew he must ignore his libido and focus on his goal. 'Are you really prepared to risk losing the Pangalos and your brother's freedom?' he asked her silkily.

The scathing look she gave him would have shrivelled another man. 'My brother is sick. His gambling addiction is out of control. What kind of terrible person are you to lend him money, knowing it would fall through his fingers? You might as well have given him a spade so that he could dig his own grave.'

Jace felt his gut clench when he saw a betraying shimmer of moisture in her eyes. 'I was not aware when I lent Mark money that he is a compulsive gambler. I simply thought he maintained an expensive lifestyle and lived beyond his means. If you knew he had a problem, why did you put him in charge of the Pangalos?'

'He told me he had stopped gambling.' She bit her lip. 'I hadn't realised how serious his problem is. My brother needs help, not a threat of prosecution.'

Jace shrugged. 'If you are serious about wanting to save him, come up to my office so that we can continue this discussion in private.'

He roamed his eyes over her flushed face and lingered on her scarlet-glossed lips. An idea of how he could fulfil his dying mother's wish—as well as his father's final plea—seeded in his mind and took root. 'I am confident we can strike a deal that will give us both what we want,' he told Eleanor.

'Will you walk into my parlour?' said the Spider to the Fly.

The line from the poem Eleanor had loved as a child popped into her head as Jace ushered her into his office. His secretary had been unable to disguise her curiosity when he had given instruction that he did not want to be disturbed for the rest of the afternoon. The snick of his office door closing made the butterflies in Eleanor's stomach flutter harder.

He held out a chair and she sank down onto it, relieved she hadn't stumbled in her four-inch heels that she was still getting used to. She grimaced when her skirt rode further up her thighs and tried to tug it down until she realised that Jace was watching her.

'You have had a change of style,' he murmured as he walked around his desk and lowered his long frame into the leather chair. 'I approve of your new look.'

Eleanor felt herself blush and silently cursed her fair skin and lack of sophistication. If only Jace wasn't so mesmerisingly sexy. His sculpted features were a work of art and the dark stubble shading his jaw accentuated his raw masculinity. A helpless longing swept through her as her gaze lingered on his mouth and she remembered the firm pressure of his lips on hers.

Although they had not had sex in the few months they had been dating, they'd indulged in heavy petting. Jace's kisses had driven her wild with desire and her breasts had ached when he'd bared them and rubbed his thumbs over her swollen nipples. A tingling sensation in that area now made Eleanor glance down, and she was mortified to see the hard points of her nipples jutting beneath her dress.

She looked up again, and as her eyes met his across the desk the predatory gleam in the dark depths of his evoked a throb of response deep in her pelvis.

'I'm sure you don't want to waste your *valuable* time discussing my appearance,' she said curtly, thinking of how he had kept her waiting. No doubt his intention had been to demonstrate that he had power over her, but she refused to be intimidated.

He leaned back in his chair and appraised her from between his narrowed gaze. 'I assume the reason for your visit is to ask for more time to try to raise the money your brother owes me. My answer is no.'

'I need three months to restructure the company's finances, and I should be able to pay back at least part of Mark's debt,' she said urgently. 'Surely you can wait three months?'

Jace's eyes glittered. 'I have waited for twenty years to take back what Kostas stole from my family.'

Eleanor stared at his hard-boned face and wondered how she had missed the ruthlessness beneath his charm a year ago. Love had blinded her, she acknowledged bitterly. Defeat tasted rancid in her mouth. 'You want fifty per cent of the Pangalos,' she muttered.

He nodded. 'But the hotel is not all I want. I've raised the stakes.'

'What else can you possibly want from me?'

'Marriage.' He met her stunned expression with a smile that bared his white teeth and reminded Eleanor of a wolf. 'I want you to marry me.'

CHAPTER THREE

'I MUST SAY that I preferred your first proposal,' Eleanor said after she had stopped laughing. Because she was sure Jace was joking. Her stupid heart had leapt when he'd mentioned marriage, but she wasn't the gullible idiot she'd been a year ago. 'Paris was much more romantic,' she mocked. 'You even gave me a sparkly ring.'

Amusement and something like admiration gleamed in his dark eyes. 'You can wear your engagement ring again once we have finalised the details of our marriage.'

The joke had gone far enough. Eleanor looked away from him, desperate to hide how much he had hurt her. 'I wouldn't marry you if the continuation of the human race depended on it.'

'In that case you had better hope your brother likes prison food.'

'Don't threaten me.' She curled her hands

into fists in her lap as a mixture of fear and fury swept through her.

'Face facts, Eleanor,' he drawled. 'I have the power to ruin Mark and force the Pangalos to be declared insolvent, meaning that lawyers will take charge of the hotel and sell off its assets to pay its creditors. I will be able to buy up the assets and I could end up owning a one hundred per cent share of the Pangalos.'

Eleanor had a business degree and knew the laws concerning a company going into liquidation. She felt sick. 'Why didn't you do that a year ago instead of going through the charade of asking me to marry you?'

He shrugged, drawing her attention to his broad shoulders sheathed in a superbly tailored charcoal-grey suit. Jace had once told her that he had started his working life as a labourer on a building site, and Eleanor guessed it was where he had developed his powerfully muscular physique.

'Your brother hadn't racked up huge debts for himself or the hotel a year ago,' he drawled. 'If we marry, the hotel will be deemed a marital asset and I will gain the fifty per cent share that my father originally owned before Kostas betrayed their friendship.'

'Are you really so cold that you would marry for such a cynical reason?' Eleanor muttered.

'I certainly wouldn't marry out of a misplaced sense of sentimentality.' Jace grimaced. 'However, my mother is a born romantic and she is desperate to see me happily married before she dies.'

Eleanor's attention was caught by the undercurrent of emotion in his voice. 'Is that likely to be soon?'

'Doctors have given her six months to a year to live.'

'I'm sorry.' She bit her lip. 'But why would us marrying make your mother happy? We don't love each other.'

'You accepted my proposal a year ago because you were in love with me,' he reminded her.

She flushed, thinking of how easily she had been taken in by his calculated seduction. 'I'm not in love with you any more, that's for sure.'

'Good,' he said coolly. 'It will make things much less complicated if we keep emotions out of our marriage.'

'I'm not going to marry you, Jace.' She stood up and looked frantically over to the door, keen to escape from this man who, even though she knew she would never mean anything to him, made her weak with longing to feel his lips on hers.

It was just her body's physical response to his magnetism, Eleanor assured herself. Jace had uncovered a sensual side to her that she'd been unaware of. In the past year she'd tried to forget how he had aroused her desire. She hadn't been remotely tempted to try to replicate the feeling with any other man. But five minutes in Jace's company had turned her into a mass of molten need.

'Why not?' he demanded in that slightly cynical, slightly amused tone of voice that made her grind her teeth.

'How can you ask that? There are a million reasons why I refuse to be your wife.'

'I can think of two very good reasons why you should consider it. Your brother's freedom and the Pangalos hotel,' he listed, his brows lifting when she shook her head.

'I'll find the money to pay back Mark's debts some other way that doesn't involve a loveless marriage to a man I despise.'

'We both know I am your brother's only hope of salvation. Sit down, Eleanor, and hear me out.'

She sat, compelled by the intensity of his gaze and his sheer force of will.

'What I am offering is a straightforward deal. Marry me and your brother's slate is wiped clean, plus I will pay all the Pangalos's outstanding bills. A prenuptial agreement will make us joint owners of the hotel and, after my mother dies, we will divorce and each receive a fifty per cent share of the business.'

'It's a crazy idea,' Eleanor muttered. She'd be even crazier to contemplate agreeing to Jace's suggestion.

'There is one other thing. My mother must not find out that you are Kostas's grand-daughter. She knows nothing about you. Your mother took your English father's name on their marriage and there is no reason why you would be associated with the name Pangalos.'

Eleanor frowned. 'Are you saying you would want your mother to think we had married for conventional reasons? I'm sure you could convince her that you are in love. After all, you fooled me,' she reminded him curtly. 'But I loathe you, and I'll never be able to pretend that you are the man of my dreams.'

She jumped up again and walked quickly towards the door. But Jace moved with the deadly speed of a panther and clamped his hand over hers on the door handle.

'Is there a man in your life who is responsible for the change in your appearance? Do you dress to please a lover?' His cool voice belied the blistering intensity in his gaze as he stared down at her from the advantage of his superior height.

'I dress to please myself,' she snapped. Her breath snagged in her throat as she breathed in his seductive male scent: spicy cologne mixed with something indefinable and uniquely Jace. 'My private life is my own affair but if, for argument's sake, I said that I have a boyfriend, you would presumably drop the idea of us marrying.'

'Not necessarily. I foresee that we would both have a certain amount of freedom within the marriage, but I'd expect you to be discreet, as I will be.'

Tears stung Eleanor's eyes, but she willed herself not to cry in front of Jace. She'd thought that he could not hurt her more than he'd already done, but she had been wrong. His detachment was a painful reminder that he had only pretended to desire her a year ago. But, in a strange way, knowing what he really thought of her would make her even more determined to ignore her sexual attraction to him—*if* she agreed to his outrageous marriage demand.

'So I would be your wife in name only?' she clarified.

'The extent of our relationship will be up to you, and I will abide by your decision.'

In other words he could take her or leave her. She was mortified by the thought that if she indicated she wanted their marriage to include sex, Jace might force himself to make love to her.

'I imagine your boyfriend was public school educated and has a job in the City, or perhaps he is a historian studying for a doctorate at one of Oxford University's illustrious colleges,' Jace drawled. 'But a *boy* will not satisfy your passionate nature, *omorfiá mou.*'

'You really are a jerk,' she spat, scarlet-faced. 'If you remember, I speak Greek and I know you don't think much of my looks. Save your false flattery for someone who is foolish enough to believe a word that comes out of your mouth.'

She hated him with every fibre of her being, but her treacherous body hadn't got the message. Eleanor could not prevent her gaze from focusing on his mouth, which he had used with such exquisite effect when he'd kissed her.

And not just on her lips. She remembered his mouth on her breasts, his wicked tongue teasing her nipples before he closed his lips around one turgid peak and then the other, making her tremble with needs that only Jace had ever aroused. Now she understood that his caresses had been part of his campaign to trick her into marriage, but even knowing the extent of his duplicity did not douse the fire inside her.

Jace's eyes glittered with anger and something else that made Eleanor's pulse accelerate when he released his grip on her fingers curled around the door handle and slid his hand beneath her chin.

'Do you think I am pretending now?' he growled. His free hand captured hers and held it against his chest so that she felt the hard thud of his heart.

The warmth of his body through his shirt evoked a flood of heat between her thighs. Her bra felt too tight, her nipples scraping against the lace cups. But she couldn't— *wouldn't*—surrender to his expert seduction again.

'It was all a game to you,' she choked.

'This was real.' His stark voice sent a shiver through her. She watched his head descend and knew she should move away from him. But another instinct as old as the story of Eve kept her standing there, waiting, willing him to close the gap between them and claim her mouth with his.

Her lips unconsciously parted and she heard

his breathing quicken. The air was heavy with sexual tension. But could she believe the hunger in Jace's eyes, or was it a continuation of the cruel game he'd started a year ago?

From outside, a clap of thunder shook the windows and shattered the fraught silence in the room. Eleanor blinked and realised that it was almost dark in Jace's office. A sudden white flash of lightning momentarily illuminated his tall figure, but his expression was hidden from her and he was a stranger.

With a low cry, she snatched her hand from his silk shirt stretched across his chest. 'I won't marry you. *I won't.* You can have fifty per cent of the Pangalos, and I'll appoint a new manager to take Mark's place so that I never have to see you again.'

This time when she grabbed the handle and opened the door, he did not try to stop her from leaving. She fought the urge to run along the corridor to the lift. When she stepped inside, before the doors closed, she looked back towards Jace's office and felt no surprise that he had not followed her. All he wanted was part ownership of the Pangalos, but she would not sign over the deeds until she had it in black and white that he would cancel her brother's debts.

To avoid the complicated one-way traffic system in Thessaloniki, Eleanor had parked her car a few streets away from Zagorakis Estates' office building. Thunder rumbled overhead as she hurried along the pavement where café owners were scrambling to carry chairs and tables inside before the furniture was blown over by the ferocious wind. Towering dark clouds obliterated the sun and the sky had turned a strange sulphur-yellow colour.

The rain started with the suddenness of a tap being turned on, and within minutes she was soaked to the skin. Cursing her high heels, she kicked off her shoes and carried them in her hand as she ran along the street. A sleek silver sports car drew up alongside her and the window slid down. Eleanor glanced at Jace behind the wheel and ran faster.

'Eleanor, get in the car.' He swore and drove on past her, stopping at a junction directly in her path. He leaned across and opened the passenger door.

'Go away!' Eleanor shouted at him over the howl of the wind.

'*Theos!* Get in the damned car!'

Hailstones mixed with the rain lashed her skin. She saw Jace's thunderous expression and decided that it was safer to obey him.

'Put your seatbelt on,' he growled when she had shut the door. Shivering, Eleanor complied, and Jace drove off. The smell of rain from her clothes and dripping-wet hair permeated the car and, looking down, she saw that her dress was clinging to her breasts. Conscious of Jace glancing at her, she folded her arms in front of her to hide her jutting nipples. He muttered something beneath his breath and switched on the car's heater.

'My car is not far from here,' she told him stiffly.

'There are reports of flash flooding on the highway, and you can't make the two-hour journey back to Sithonia in wet clothes. I'll take you to my house so that you can dry off.' Without giving her a chance to argue, he continued, 'Why did you run off like that when the storm was about to break?'

Eleanor wondered if he was referring to the

weather phenomenon or the tempest that had brewed between them in his office. 'I can't marry you,' she muttered.

'Is that because you have a romantic ideal of what marriage should be?'

Stung by his cynicism, she said defensively, 'I believe in marrying for love. My grandparents were married for fifty years before Nanna Francine died. My parents were happily married, and the only thing that made their deaths more bearable was knowing they were together at the end.'

She was aware of Jace's brooding gaze on her before he turned his attention back to the road. The driving conditions were terrible, and the windscreen wipers could hardly cope with the heavy rain.

'I remember you mentioned that your parents died in an accident when you were a child.'

'They were on a second honeymoon to celebrate their twentieth wedding anniversary. Someone noticed my mother get into difficulties while she was swimming in the sea. Dad went to help her, and they were both swept away by the strong current. Their bodies were found washed up on a beach two days later.'

'It was tough to lose one parent when I was a teenager and I can only imagine how devastating it must have been when you were orphaned.' The gruff sympathy in Jace's voice curled around Eleanor's heart.

'Mark struggled the most to come to terms with what happened. He didn't get on with my grandfather.'

'But you did, presumably, and that's why Kostas made you his heir.'

Eleanor sighed. 'He was quite controlling, and my brother and sister were argumentative, so there were clashes. I think Pappoús liked me because I tended to agree with him to keep the peace.'

She had spent much of her childhood feeling that she was a disappointment to her parents because of her scoliosis. After they had died, she'd realised that she could win her grandfather's approval and affection by being obedient and amenable.

Sometimes it felt as if she had spent her whole life trying to please people, Eleanor thought. It had not been her choice to be made her grandfather's heir and have the responsibility of Gilpin Leisure thrust upon her. And now, to save the Pangalos and her brother, Jace had demanded that she must marry him. But it would be a fake marriage, just as their romance a year ago had been fake, on his side at least.

She was jolted from her thoughts when Jace drove through a set of cobalt-blue iron gates and stopped in front of a whitewashed villa, built in the Cycladic style synonymous with the architecture of the Aegean islands. Through the torrential rain, Eleanor saw that the house resembled a series of cubes with flat roofs and arched windows framed by shutters of brilliant blue.

'The back of the house overlooks the sea, and on a clear day you can see the peninsular of Kassandra and beyond it, across the bay, Mount Olympus. But not today,' Jace said with a grimace. He slipped off his jacket and draped it around Eleanor's shoulders before he climbed out of the car and strode round to open the passenger door. Eleanor gasped as the wind whipped her breath away and drove stinging rain into her face. Jace caught hold of her hand and they ran towards the house.

When they were inside and Jace closed the front door the sound of the storm was muffled by the thick walls. Eleanor looked around the vast entrance hall with a white marble floor. Through an open door she could see a living room where a frail-looking woman was lying on a sofa.

'Jace, thank goodness you are back,' the woman spoke in Greek. 'There are news reports that power lines and trees have been brought down by the gale.' She noticed Eleanor. 'Oh, you have brought a guest home.'

'Stay where you are,' Jace commanded as the woman attempted to stand up. He put his hand beneath Eleanor's elbow and drew her forwards. 'This is my mother, Iliana. Mamá, I'd like you to meet Eleanor Buchanan. She is English but she speaks Greek fluently.'

Eleanor felt self-conscious that she was still wearing Jace's jacket around her shoulders, but at least it covered her dress, which was sticking to her body like a second skin. Jace's shirt had taken the brunt of the rain and it clung to his torso so that his black chest hairs were visible through the damp silk.

She tore her gaze from him and stepped closer to the sofa. '*Kalispera*,' she murmured as she shook hands with his mother. Iliana was painfully thin and the skin on her bony hand felt papery. The signs of illness were on her tired face, but her dark eyes gleamed with warmth and curiosity as she studied Eleanor.

'You have a beautiful name.'

'Thank you. My grandfather chose it.' Eleanor froze and dared not glance at Jace, who had tensed when she'd unthinkingly mentioned her grandfather. There was no reason why she shouldn't speak of Kostas Pangalos just because Jace had warned her not to, she told herself. She had only heard his version of an alleged feud between his father and her grandfather. But if there *was* any truth in the story she did not wish to upset Jace's fragile-looking mother.

Eleanor shivered, feeling chilled to the bone in her wet dress. Iliana immediately looked concerned. 'You must go and get dry. Will you stay to dinner?'

'Eleanor will have to spend the night here,'

Jace answered before she could speak, flashing the phone he held. 'News reports say the storm is set to last until the morning.' He placed his hand in the small of her back and steered her towards the door. 'Come with me and I'll find you something to wear.'

How had she ended up in the enemy's camp? Eleanor wondered ruefully as she followed Jace up the grand staircase. He strode along the landing on the second floor and opened a door into a charming guest bedroom decorated in the same simple style as the rest of the house, with white walls and blue shutters at the windows.

'The bathroom is through here.' He opened another door into an en suite bathroom. 'A shower will warm you up. I'll take your clothes to be laundered.'

Eleanor was so cold that her teeth chattered. 'Do you need me to help you undress?' Jace asked.

'Pigs will fly before I'll allow you to take my clothes off.'

His sexy grin stole her breath. She hated how her heart performed a somersault just because when Jace smiled he reminded her of the charismatic, irresistible man she had fallen in love with a year ago.

'Keep telling yourself that, *pouláki mou,*' he drawled.

'Don't call me that,' she muttered. 'I heard you say to Takis Samaras that my sister is a beautiful peacock, but you think I am an unremarkable sparrow. If Lissa had inherited the Pangalos, no doubt you would have been keen to marry *her.*'

Jace gave her a thoughtful look. 'Your sister is attractive, and she seems to have made a career out of dating rich male celebrities. I have met dozens of Lissas, but I've never met anyone as unique or as beautiful as you.'

Eleanor shook her head. 'You don't have to try to win me over with pretty lies any more,' she told him with quiet dignity before she walked into the bathroom and locked the door behind her.

When she emerged from the shower ten minutes later and wrapped a towel tightly around her body before cautiously stepping into the bedroom, she discovered that Jace had left one of his shirts for her to wear. Her layered hairstyle took minutes to dry with a hairdryer. The shorter length was sexier than when she'd worn her hair in a school-girlish plait, Eleanor decided. Had that unconsciously been her aim when she'd decided on a makeover of her hair and clothes? she wondered. Had she hoped to make Jace sit up and notice her?

She studied her reflection in the mirror. The borrowed shirt came down to her mid-thigh and was just about presentable to wear to dinner. She grimaced at the hectic flush on her cheeks and her dilated pupils that were evidence of the effect Jace had on her. A knock on the door made her heart skip a beat, but she was greeted by a maid who had come to show her the way to the dining room.

Although it was early in the evening the storm had turned the sky as dark as night, and lamps had been switched on in the house. When Eleanor entered the dining room her gaze was immediately drawn to Jace. He had changed out of his wet clothes and looked divine in black jeans hugging his lean hips and a fine-knit black sweater that moulded the defined ridges of his abdominal muscles.

She forced herself to walk further into the

room, conscious of his gaze roaming over her legs all the way down to her red stiletto heel shoes before moving up to the rest of her body. Could he tell that she was braless? She had draped her underwear over the heated towel rail while she showered, but only her knickers had dried enough to wear.

'Like I said, uniquely beautiful,' Jace murmured as he strolled towards her.

Eleanor opened her mouth to tell him to *stop*. How could he lie so glibly? Did he not possess an iota of compunction? But her angry words died before she uttered them when she recognised stark hunger in his eyes.

Desire. For her. A nerve flickered in his jaw and her heart pounded as she realised with a jolt of shock that he wasn't pretending. Jace wanted her with the same fierce need that she felt for him. The knowledge restored a little of her pride. The glittering intensity in his gaze put them on an equal footing, and she could not restrain a shiver of reaction.

'Do please come and sit down, Eleanor,' Jace's mother invited.

Belatedly, Eleanor realised that she and Jace were not alone. Snatching oxygen into her lungs, she whirled away from him at the same time as he stepped back from her and raked his fingers through his hair.

A maid arrived with a trolley and proceeded to serve dinner. Jace held out a chair for Eleanor and when she was seated he took his place at the head of the table. There were two bottles of wine on the table, a red and a white. He half filled his mother's glass with white wine and poured Eleanor a glass of Pinot Noir. Her eyes met his, and she told herself not to read anything into the fact that he had remembered she did not like white wine.

Across the table his mother gave her a curious look. 'Have you known my son long?'

'Um…'

'Eleanor and I met more than a year ago,' Jace murmured when she hesitated.

'A year! Well, I am delighted to finally be introduced to you.' Iliana gave a rueful smile when Eleanor's eyes rested on a large purple bruise on her face. 'I tripped over in the garden while I was trying to prune the bougainvillea,' she explained. 'Unfortunately, I'm not as agile as I used to be.'

'I employ a gardener so that you can sit

and enjoy the garden,' Jace admonished his mother gently.

'I like to do what I can. But I am embarrassed to admit that I called Jace at his office this afternoon and cried like a baby,' Iliana told Eleanor.

She darted a look at Jace. Had he been unable to keep her appointment time because he'd been comforting his mother after her accident? His closed expression gave nothing away. She looked down at her plate of moussaka. The food was delicious but she barely noticed what she was eating, feeling guilty when she remembered how she had stormed out of his office, convinced that he'd been toying with her like a cat with a mouse.

'I saw on the news programme that the storm caused a tidal surge and many properties on the coast have been damaged,' Iliana commented.

Eleanor's heart sank. The last thing she needed was a pile more bills if the hotel had suffered damage.

'I hope your accommodation hasn't been affected. Are you staying in Thessaloniki?'

'No, on Sithonia, at the…um… Pangalos

Beach Resort.' Eleanor dared not look at Jace after she had spoken unthinkingly again.

Iliana's expression was wistful. 'I have not been there for many years, but I've heard that the facilities are excellent. My husband used to partly own the hotel, and we lived there until Dimitri's business partner cheated us out of our livelihood.'

'Goodness, what happened?' Eleanor feigned surprise and ignored Jace's warning stare.

'Dimitri's partner, Kostas Pangalos, wanted to sell the Pangorakis,' Iliana explained. 'My husband could just about afford to buy the other fifty per cent, but Kostas claimed that he had done more to make the hotel successful. In court, his lawyers persuaded the judge to award Kostas two-thirds of the business and Dimitri was only given one third.'

Iliana sighed. 'The decision gave control of the hotel to Kostas and he bought my husband out. It was heartbreaking to have to leave our home and the hotel that we loved and where Jace had lived his whole life. We opened another hotel, but Dimitri's heart was not in it. He was deeply upset that the man he had considered to be his best friend had turned on him. But I was not so surprised. I always thought that beneath Kostas's charming manner he was utterly ruthless.'

'I suppose it's necessary to be fairly ruthless to be successful in business,' Eleanor murmured. She felt sick at hearing what her grandfather had done, but she had no reason to disbelieve Jace's mother.

'Kostas destroyed my husband,' Iliana said flatly. 'Our second hotel did not do well and, in desperation, Dimitri asked his old friend for a loan. Kostas could afford it. His wife had inherited a top hotel in England and the Pangalos, as he renamed our hotel, was making a fortune. But he turned Dimitri's request down and we were declared bankrupt. Soon after, my husband took his own life.'

'We don't know that for sure, Mamá,' Jace said softly. 'The inquest was inconclusive, and it could have been an accident.'

Iliana shook her head. 'Your father did not stumble and fall off the cliff. His heart was broken, and Kostas Pangalos was responsible for his death as much as if he had pushed Dimitri over the edge.'

CHAPTER FOUR

JACE STOOD IN the orangery and watched the rain lash against the glass. He had not switched on the lamps and the room was illuminated sporadically when the moon appeared from behind clouds scudding across the night sky.

He sipped his whisky. Listening to his mother's account of how Kostas had destroyed his father had reinforced Jace's determination to claim his family's rightful share of the Pangalos. But he had taken no pleasure in Eleanor's obvious shock. She had managed to hide her distress from his mother, but not from him. He'd heard a tremor in her voice when immediately after dinner she'd made an excuse that she had a headache before going to her room.

Lying did not come naturally to Eleanor, Jace brooded. She was the most guileless and honest person he had ever met. He remembered her shy smile a year ago when she'd confessed that she had fallen in love with him. Instead of feeling triumphant that his plan to claim the hotel was coming to fruition, he had admired her bravery and felt uncomfortable with himself.

But when he'd kissed her and passion had exploded between them he had told himself that Eleanor had mistaken lust for a deeper emotion. Now he believed her when she said she hated him. It was an inescapable fact that if she had not discovered his motive for proposing to her in Paris he would have married her for the Pangalos.

A faint sound from behind him made Jace turn his head and he watched Eleanor walk barefoot into the orangery. She did not notice him standing in the shadows as she crossed to the window and stared out at the dark garden. His gaze lingered on her delectable curves, which he could make out beneath his borrowed shirt, and his body clenched hard as desire ran like wildfire through his veins. Where once her sensual allure had been muted, her transformation into a sexy siren evoked a throb of need that centred in his groin.

'Headache gone?' he murmured.

She spun round and he heard her swiftly indrawn breath. 'I didn't see you there.'

'I guessed as much,' Jace said wryly. 'You made it clear when you disappeared after dinner that you would rather spend time with the devil than with me.'

'I couldn't sleep.' She turned away from him and hugged her arms around her body. 'I'm sorry for what my grandfather did to your family.' Her voice sounded raw, as if she had swallowed broken glass. 'Pappoús...' She swallowed audibly. 'When I was growing up, I thought he was firm but fair and... I loved him. But now I wonder if I ever knew him. The man who treated me kindly was the same man who cheated your father.' She drew in a ragged breath. 'I understand now why you must hate me.'

'I don't hate you,' Jace growled. 'I hated Kostas and I want my father's rightful share of the Pangalos, but I wish you hadn't been caught up in an old feud between our families that had nothing to do with you.'

'Why didn't you tell me when we first met?'

Eleanor jerked her head in his direction and her eyes flashed in the darkness.

'I couldn't risk it. Kostas had chosen you as his heir, but I knew nothing about you. You might have been as ruthless as your grandfather and refused to hand over my father's share of the hotel.'

'So you deliberately set out to make me fall in love with you.' She bit her lip. 'Your treatment of me was as cruel as anything Pappoús did.'

'Kostas destroyed my family,' Jace growled angrily. His blissful childhood with his parents had ended abruptly when they were forced to leave the hotel and they had been homeless and without hope. Life had been different after that, as his father struggled with depression and his mother had scrubbed floors for a pittance. Jace had spent years plotting and planning to destroy Kostas, but now the old man was dead and he had left his granddaughter to succeed him.

A year ago Jace had been prepared to destroy Eleanor, but his conscience pricked that she had not deserved what he had done to her. Only now did he acknowledge how cruelly he had betrayed her. Without conscious thought, he strode across the room and halted in front of her. The seductive fragrance of her perfume assailed his senses and his gut clenched.

'You ripped my heart out and made a fool of me, and I will never forgive you,' she whispered.

He swore when he glimpsed the shimmer of tears in her eyes. In the near darkness, with the storm still raging outside, he sensed that her emotions were heightened, as were his. Jace was strongly tempted to kiss the stubborn line of Eleanor's mouth until her lips softened. But giving in to his clamouring libido would complicate the situation even more, he reminded himself.

'I don't need your forgiveness,' he told her curtly. 'All I want is your signature on a marriage certificate.'

'You can't be serious about wanting to marry me when there is so much animosity between us. You could have any woman you want.' Eleanor blushed when Jace raised his brows. 'Don't be coy,' she muttered. 'You know you're a catch.'

'Money tends to do that,' he said drily.

'I'm sure you are well aware of the effect you have on the female sex.'

'I'm interested to know what effect I have on you.'

She met his gaze steadily and Jace experienced the unfamiliar sensation of being judged and found wanting. 'I think you are beautiful but flawed,' Eleanor told him. 'I've seen inside your soul and there's nothing there but an empty void.'

He shrugged. But he was stung by her evaluation of him. 'That is why you will be my perfect temporary wife, *omorfiá mou*. You won't harbour hopes that I will fall in love with you.'

'No, I won't make that mistake again, Jace.' Eleanor's voice was as dry as a desert. She sighed. 'During dinner, when you went to your study to take a business call, your mother told me how hard life was for both of you after your father died. She said you had to leave school early and get a job.' Eleanor hesitated. 'Your mother also mentioned that you deserved to be lucky after something terrible happened to you.'

Jace stiffened. This was an opportunity to

tell Eleanor that he had served a prison sentence. But he balked at trying to explain that his conviction for assault had been unjust and he had acted in self-defence. A judge hadn't believed his version of what had happened, so why would Eleanor? Grimly, he acknowledged that he had done nothing to earn her trust.

'Ah,' he murmured, as if he'd just realised what his mother had meant. 'I believed I was in love once, but my girlfriend dumped me for a richer man. I suppose it seemed terrible at the time, but I had the last laugh when I won a million euros on a lottery game.'

Eleanor looked startled. 'Did you try to persuade your girlfriend back with your winnings?'

'No, I used the money to establish a property development business. It was a safer bet than Katerina, who had shown that she was a gold-digger,' Jace said sardonically. 'It was the first ticket I'd ever bought and, unlike your brother, I knew that the odds of another big win if I gambled again were minuscule. The money gave me the opportunity to do something with my life. I worked hard, and within five years my business portfolio was worth twenty times my original win.'

He had clawed his way to the top. Kostas's betrayal of his father had taught him never to trust anyone, Jace brooded. He was proud of everything he had achieved.

'Now you are reputed to be one of the wealthiest men in Greece,' Eleanor murmured. 'But I have the one thing you want but cannot buy.'

She released a shaky breath. 'Your mother told me that she would be overjoyed to see you married before she dies. My brother talked of ending his life because he is worried about his debts. So I'll marry you, and you will gain fifty per cent of the Pangalos. More importantly, we will be able to help the people we care about. But our marriage will be a business arrangement, as you suggested. For your mother's sake I will pretend to be your loving wife in public, but in private we will lead separate lives. Discreetly, of course,' she added coolly.

It was exactly what Jace had wanted. A marriage that would make his mother happy in the last months of her life and secure him half-ownership of the Pangalos. He should feel exultant, but he was infuriated to hear Eleanor state in a prim voice, so at odds with her sex siren looks, that she wanted an open marriage.

Did she have some guy in the background? Jace wondered furiously. He gritted his teeth at the idea that once Eleanor was his wife she might plan to slip out of the marital home to spend nights or maybe weekends with a lover. Yes, such an arrangement could work in his favour too. But he had not slept with a woman since before he'd met Eleanor fifteen months ago. The realisation made him frown. He did not want a mistress. He wanted his eager bride of a year ago.

Jace remembered how his body had been taut with anticipation at the prospect of taking Eleanor to bed in Paris. He had been turned on by her beguiling mix of innocence and sensuality. The way she was looking at him now, with a hungry desire that turned her hazel eyes green, shook his resolve to keep his hands off her.

'You can forget about us having an open marriage,' he told her bluntly. 'I won't stand for you flaunting your affairs with other men while you are my wife.'

She looked confused and then angry. 'It was your idea. You said we would both have freedom within the marriage.'

Jace was irritated that she quoted him, and he tried to recall what other crass things he might have said. 'I am a well-known figure in Greece, and the media take excessive interest in my personal life. It would be deeply upsetting for my mother if she heard rumours that we were not committed to our marriage.'

He stared down at Eleanor and felt a curious tug in his chest as he roamed his gaze over the delicate contours of her face. It amazed him that he had overlooked her English rose beauty initially. Her eyes darkened, the pupils dilating so they were fathomless black pools ringed by irises that had turned as green as a stormy sea. He knew she felt the simmering awareness between them, and when her tongue darted across her bottom lip it took all Jace's willpower not to sweep her into his arms and crush her mouth beneath his.

'You have a reputation as a playboy. Do you expect me to believe that you will remain celibate during our marriage?' Her hair swirled in a fragrant cloud around her shoulders when she shook her head. She gave him a belligerent look as she placed her hands on her hips.

The action drew Jace's attention to her breasts rising and falling quickly beneath the shirt he'd lent her. The outline of her nipples through the thin cotton answered the question that had plagued him throughout dinner. She wasn't wearing a bra and he felt his body respond to the invitation she was throwing out.

'I have no intention of living like a monk,' he drawled. Her indignant expression brought a mocking smile to his lips. 'Don't go there, *omorfiá mou*,' he warned softly. 'I certainly won't force you to have sex with me, if that was the accusation you were about to make. But I guarantee that at some point our marriage will include a sexual relationship.'

She took a deep breath that made her breasts swell so that the buttons down the front of the shirt appeared to be in danger of pinging open. 'You are *so* arrogant.'

'And you are a pretty little liar if you deny that you want this,' Jace said roughly. He could no longer fight his desire for Eleanor that pumped powerfully through his veins. When he slipped his hand beneath her chin and tilted her face to his he saw the same urgent excitement in her eyes that consumed him. But he forced himself to hold back.

'I am not restraining you in any way,' he murmured. 'You are free to leave. But if you don't move in the next ten seconds, I give you fair warning that I am going to kiss you.'

'*Go on then.*'

The words slipped out of Eleanor's mouth before she could stop them. She felt herself blush, but she stared at Jace's heartbreakingly handsome face as he lowered his head towards her and her feet refused to budge. There was no chance she would fall in love with him again, she assured herself. He was a lying toad and she hated him, but she craved his kiss.

Who was she kidding? She wanted more than his kisses. She had been startled by his accusation that she might want affairs with other men. Jace was the only man she wanted. A year ago he had given her a glimpse of her own sensuality and her body felt cheated that she had not experienced the sexual fulfilment his caresses had promised.

He moved his hand up and cupped her cheek, brushing his thumb lightly over her sensitised skin. The oddly tender gesture caused her heart to slam headlong into her ribcage. She snatched a breath seconds before he grazed his mouth across hers. The effect was electrifying. Every cell in her body quivered with acute awareness of him and with a need she did not fully understand but it made her tremble and shift closer to him.

Jace groaned and lashed his arm around her waist, pulling her against the muscled hardness of his thighs. And Eleanor melted. Any lingering thoughts of resistance disappeared as she responded to Jace's demands with a helplessness that would have appalled hcr if she had been capable of rational logic. There would be time for self-recrimination later. Now there was simply fire and flame as Jace licked his way into her mouth and tangled his tongue with hers.

He tasted of smoky whisky and Eleanor felt as if she had come home. His mouth fitted hers perfectly and his fierce passion eased a little the hurt he had inflicted on her heart a year ago. He slid his hand into her hair and angled her head while he deepened the kiss and it became an erotic feast.

With a soft moan, Eleanor wound her arms around his neck and pressed herself against his whipcord body. This was what she had dreamed of night after night since she had fled from him in Paris. Jace was her master and she became alive beneath his magician's touch.

Compelled by feminine instinct and a desperation to be even closer to him, she slipped her hands beneath the hem of his sweater and discovered the tantalising warmth of his bare skin. Her fingertips explored the ridges of his abdominal muscles before moving up to skim across the whorls of hair that grew on his chest.

Touching him wasn't enough. She wanted to see him. She must have spoken her thoughts aloud because he gave a rough laugh and yanked his sweater over his head with clumsy haste rather than his usual grace.

Outside, the storm had cleared, leaving a white moon to cast a pearlescent gleam into the orangery and over Jace's half-naked body. He could have been a sculpture by Michelangelo but, unlike cold marble, his skin felt warm to Eleanor's lips when she kissed the place above where his heart thudded unevenly.

He growled something unintelligible and seized her in his arms once more, bringing his mouth down on hers and kissing her with untrammelled passion. His fingers deftly unfastened the buttons on her shirt and Eleanor felt a tiny stab of jealousy at the evidence of his expertise at undressing women. But when he parted the edges of the shirt and bared her breasts, setting her away from him so that he could look at her, his husky groan evoked a throb of desire between her legs.

'*Eísai ómorfi,*' Jace said in a strained voice. He repeated in English, 'You are beautiful.'

The hot gleam of desire in his eyes made Eleanor *feel* beautiful. Whatever had happened in the past, *this* now was real. The slight unsteadiness of Jace's hand when he reached out and cupped her breast told her that it was not a calculated seduction. The chemistry smouldering between them was too strong for either of them to resist.

She caught her breath when he stroked his thumb across her nipple and brought it to a tingling, hard peak. With a soft sigh, she arched towards him and he claimed her lips once more in a shockingly sensual kiss that plundered her soul. Eleanor was conscious only of Jace, his mouth wreaking havoc and his caresses increasingly bold as he trailed his fingertips over her stomach, down to her knickers, where the lacy panel between her legs was damp with her arousal. Nothing mattered but that he should assuage the insistent ache there.

A sudden, shocking bright light replaced the pale gleam of the moon. Eleanor stiffened as Jace tore his lips from hers and cursed beneath his breath. He narrowed his eyes against the glare of the overhead light.

'Is something wrong, Mamá? Do you feel ill?'

Iliana was standing in the doorway and looked embarrassed. But Eleanor was even more mortified and hastily tugged the shirt over her breasts.

'*Sygnómi,*' his mother apologised. 'I thought I had left my reading glasses in here and I did not want to disturb Anna. But I have disturbed you.'

'You may as well hear our news, Mamá,' Jace said softly. 'We were going to tell you in the morning.' He draped his arm around Eleanor's shoulders and smiled down at her. The warning glint in his eyes jolted her back to reality and reminded her that once again he was only pretending to be in love with her. But this time she was part of the pretence and she gave him a saccharine-sweet smile.

He stared at her intently as if he were trying to read her mind. Let him try, she thought. A year ago she had worn her heart on her sleeve, but now she was wary and determined that he would not hurt her again.

'Eleanor has agreed to be my wife,' Jace told his mother. 'We are going to be married. Not only that, but earlier today I finalised a deal which will return my father's share of the Pangalos hotel to the Zagorakis family.'

Iliana looked stunned for a moment before her lined face broke into a joyous smile. 'My prayers have been answered. Everything I hoped for has come true, and when I take my last breath I will be at peace.' She clasped Eleanor's hand. 'I see tenderness in the way my son looks at you. And you love him, don't you?'

Eleanor hesitated and her gaze flew to Jace's inscrutable expression. She had a better understanding of why he had cold-heartedly seduced her a year ago. He had loved his father and now he wanted to make his mother happy before she died. Jace wasn't completely heartless. Before they had been interrupted, his desire for her had been real. She'd felt the hard proof of his arousal against her hip. But he would never fall in love with Kostas Pangalos's granddaughter and she must not forget it.

'Jace knows how I feel about him,' she murmured, and wondered why he frowned.

Bright sunshine on an English summer's day poured through Eleanor's office window at Francine's hotel and set the enormous diamond on her finger ablaze.

'That's quite a rock.' Her sister sounded envious.

Eleanor sighed. Her engagement ring was certainly eye-catching and must be worth a fortune. When Jace had returned the ring to her before she'd left Greece two weeks ago its sparkling brilliance had been a mocking reminder that the diamond solitaire held no emotional significance. The truth was that she would have preferred a less showy ring. Perhaps she was more like a brown sparrow than a peacock, as Jace had once described her, she thought ruefully.

'You are a dark horse,' Lissa said. 'How did you manage to persuade one of the richest and sexiest men in Europe to marry you? I wasn't aware that you knew Jace Zagorakis until I read the announcement of your engagement in the newspaper. You might have told me first.'

To Eleanor's surprise her sister sounded hurt. 'There wasn't time,' she explained hurriedly. 'Jace wants us to marry as soon as possible because his mother is ill. He made the press announcement on the same day that notice of our marriage was published in a local Greek newspaper, which is the rule before we could apply for a wedding licence.'

She looked back at her computer screen, frowning when she thought of the amount of work she still had to do. Jace had tried to persuade her to stay at his house in Thessaloniki for the month leading up to their wedding, but she'd insisted on returning to Oxford. She had things to sort out, she'd told him. But the real reason was that she hadn't trusted herself to live in close proximity to Jace. Their separation was a chance for her to build her defences against his charisma but, annoyingly, he invaded her dreams every night.

As well as a lack of sleep, Eleanor had been dealing with numerous issues at the Oxford hotel. A serious leak in one of the upstairs bathrooms had flooded two of the newly refurbished suites, which had incurred more expense. She'd had no time to prepare for her move to Greece, and hadn't even bought a wedding dress yet.

'I can't believe that Craig has decided to relocate to Canada,' she groaned. 'I had intended to promote him to General Manager of Francine's. I'll keep my position as Vice President of Operations, but I will be living in Halkidiki and involved with running the

Pangalos. I want to feel confident that I'm leaving Francine's in good hands, but none of the applicants I've interviewed for the GM role have been right.'

'You could give the position to me.' Lissa grimaced when Eleanor stared at her. 'I know you think that I spend my life going to parties but, as a matter of fact, I went to college in London and studied for a diploma in hotel management. For the last six months I've worked in a management role at the Bainbridge Hotel in Mayfair. It was only a junior position, but I'm capable of running Francine's if you would give me the chance.'

'But you were never interested in the hotel.'

'I was always interested, but when I asked Pappoús if he would give me a trial job so that I could prove I was prepared to work hard, he refused. You were the chosen one,' Lissa said bitterly. 'Pappoús didn't think much of me and Mark. It was always Eleanor with her business degree. Eleanor who never disagreed with him. You were his favourite because you reminded him of Mum.'

Eleanor thought of her beautiful, elegant mother. 'I'm not a bit like her.'

Lissa nodded. 'You have the same serene air that Mum had. And now that you've ditched those awful granny cardigans and got a new hairstyle you look amazing.' She grinned at Eleanor's shocked expression. 'You look like a woman in love.'

Eleanor was tempted to confide to her sister the real reason why she was marrying Jace. She certainly wasn't in love with him, she assured herself. But during his nightly phone calls he was charming and amusing and seemed genuinely interested in what she had to say. She had found herself relaxing and opening up to him as she'd done when he had courted her fifteen months ago.

Memories of his passionate kisses in Greece on the night of the storm were rarely out of her mind. Jace had made it clear that he would not force her into his bed. If they had not been interrupted she would have made love with him because she couldn't resist him, Eleanor thought ruefully. Why shouldn't she take what Jace was offering? whispered a voice of temptation in her head. She wanted to have sex with him, but she would not confuse lust for love, and she was strong enough to walk away from him when the fire between them died.

'Please give me a chance.' Lissa's voice pulled Eleanor back to the present.

She frowned, remembering how Mark had said the same thing. But her little sister had grown up and was a stronger character than their brother. Eleanor was shocked that Lissa had been jealous of her relationship with their grandfather. 'I thought you wanted to be an actress,' she murmured.

'I realised in California that I don't have enough talent. And I refused to sleep with the film director who invited me to dinner to discuss a possible role in his film.' Lissa gave her a pleading look. 'I won't let you down.'

'Well… Craig doesn't go to Canada for two months. You could shadow him and…'

'Oh, thanks, El.' Lissa beamed. 'You won't regret it. Now you can stop worrying about Francine's and get on with preparations for your wedding.' She picked up a bridal magazine from Eleanor's desk. 'Have you chosen a wedding dress?'

'Not yet. What do you think of the one on the front cover?'

Her sister shook her head. 'It will make you look like a meringue. She flicked through the pages and showed Eleanor an overtly sexy fitted gown with a plunging neckline and a fishtail skirt. 'This would suit you. If you wear a dress like this on your wedding day, your hunky fiancé will be impatient to rip it off you.'

Eleanor could not restrain a little shiver as she imagined Jace's hands caressing her body on their wedding night. 'Will you come shopping with me?' she asked Lissa. 'I need to buy a trousseau and I'd appreciate your advice.'

CHAPTER FIVE

FOLLOWING THE SATNAV'S instructions, Jace drove along a narrow lane on the outskirts of Oxford and through a gate into a field. Although it was early in the morning, a crowd of people were milling about. Not for the first time he asked himself why he had interrupted his flight back to Greece from New York, where he'd had a series of business meetings, and instructed his pilot to make a stopover in England.

On the passenger seat of his car was a bouquet of pink roses that he had impulsively bought at the airport for Eleanor. Jace never did anything by impulse. He planned every aspect of his life with calculated detachment, and in the past when he'd given flowers to a lover his PA had ordered them from a florist.

He frowned as he recalled his conversation with Eleanor's sister when he'd arrived at Francine's hotel. Lissa had looked at him curiously. 'Eleanor has gone to a balloon event with her friend Nigel and she left me in charge of the hotel for the weekend. I'm going to be the General Manager of Francine's after my sister marries you and moves to Greece,' Lissa had said with pride in her voice.

Perhaps Lissa Buchanan wasn't as superficial as his first opinion of her, Jace had mused before he'd dismissed Eleanor's sister from his mind. He hadn't understood what Lissa had meant by a balloon event, but as he drove across the field he saw that people were grouped around hot-air balloons which were being inflated. He had no idea why Eleanor had got up at the crack of dawn to watch balloons. More to the point, what was the exact nature of her relationship with 'her friend' who she planned to spend the weekend with? Jace wondered as he parked the car and strolled over to some people.

'Sure, Eleanor is here with Nigel. They never miss a club event,' someone told Jace, pointing to a blue and white balloon.

He headed across the field in the direction of the group standing around a wicker basket attached to a striped balloon. His steps slowed when he spotted Eleanor and he felt an inexplicable tug in his chest as he studied her. She was delectable in tight-fitting jeans and a bubblegum-pink tee shirt that moulded her high, firm breasts. Her hair was caught in a loose knot on top of her head and she looked natural and wholesome, and at the same time achingly desirable.

Jace's attention had been riveted on Eleanor, but he shifted his gaze to the lanky guy with hair flopping into his eyes who she was with. Eleanor was smiling as she chatted animatedly to the guy. Suddenly she threw her arms around his neck and the two of them hugged.

Jace was unprepared for the sensation of an iron band wrapping around his chest and squeezing the air out of his lungs. A lead weight dropped into his stomach and there was a bitter taste in his mouth. He might have suspected that what he was feeling was jealousy if the idea wasn't laughable. Since Katerina had shown her true colours many years ago, he hadn't allowed himself to get close to any woman on an emotional level and he kept his affairs purely physical.

Eleanor had been different. Their courtship had been gentle but with simmering chemistry below the surface. Jace acknowledged that it was not surprising if she had replaced him in her affections with a new boyfriend. But seeing her wrapped around Mr Floppy-Hair infuriated him. She had agreed to marry *him,* and part of the deal was that neither of them would stray outside of the marriage.

Jace dismissed as irrelevant the fact that Eleanor was not his wife yet. Their wedding was in a week's time. He had put a diamond the size of a rock on her finger, and he had every right to demand to know what the hell was going on.

He strode across the dew-damp grass, frowning as he watched Eleanor climb into the basket, above which the balloon was now inflated. The guy she had been hugging climbed into the basket with her.

'Jace!' Her eyes widened when she saw him. 'What are you doing here? I wasn't expecting you to come to Oxford.'

'Evidently not,' he drawled, looking pointedly from Eleanor to her companion.

'This is Nigel.' She looked puzzled when

Jace hooked his leg over the side of the wicker basket. 'You can't come in. There is only room for two people.'

'In that case one of us will have to get out.' He glowered at the other man.

'I'll leave you to it,' Nigel said hurriedly and climbed out of the basket.

Jace decided that if looks could kill, the glare Eleanor directed at him would make him a dead man.

'What was that about?' she demanded frostily.

His eyes narrowed on her flushed cheeks and his body reacted predictably to the sight of her breasts rising and falling swiftly beneath her tight tee shirt. 'Is Mr Floppy your lover?'

'Mr Flop…? Oh, you mean Nigel. He's a friend, nothing more.'

'You were plastered all over him.'

Her breath hissed between her teeth. 'He had just told me that his wife is expecting their first baby after several years of trying to get pregnant. I'm really happy for Nigel and Clare. How *dare* you behave like a possessive jerk?'

Jace was intrigued by Eleanor's outburst of temper. A year ago she had kept her passionate nature hidden from him, or maybe he had not taken the time to discover the real woman behind her rather bland shell. There was nothing bland about her now, he brooded, his eyes fixed on her moist lips as her tongue darted over them.

'Eleanor, are you ready to launch?' Nigel called out.

'Ready,' Eleanor shouted above the noise of the burner that was shooting flames into the mouth of the canopy.

Jace tensed when he realised that the balloon was rising into the air and the crew had let go of the ropes which had secured the basket to the ground. 'Do you actually mean to go up in this thing?' He watched Eleanor fiddling with the burner equipment. 'Surely we need someone with us who knows what they're doing?'

'I *do* know what I'm doing. I'm a qualified balloon pilot.'

'*You?*'

'Why are you so shocked?'

He blew out a breath. 'I didn't know you were a fan of dangerous sports.'

'Ballooning isn't dangerous when it's done properly.' She held his gaze and Jace looked away first when she said drily, 'You never really knew me.'

After a moment, Eleanor said, 'I gained my balloon pilot's licence a while ago. The weather is unpredictable in England, so I went to a flight training school in Turkey and did a crash course.'

The ground was a long way down. Jace took a deep breath. 'That's not funny.'

'What? Oh, sorry, no pun intended.' She stared at him. 'Are you okay?'

'I'm not a fan of heights,' he gritted, his jaw clenched.

'But you own your own jet and regularly fly across the world for business.'

'I trust my pilot.'

'Well, like it or not, you'll have to trust me. I'm going to turn the burner off now that we have reached the right altitude.'

The silence that enveloped them was like nothing Jace had ever experienced before.

'Look at the view,' Eleanor urged him. 'Isn't it incredible?'

The Oxfordshire countryside was spread beneath them, a patchwork of fields criss-crossed with green hedges and the silver glint of the river. But Jace still felt ill at ease. 'Where are we going?'

'Wherever the wind takes us. There is no way of steering the balloon. The only control the pilot has is altitude. We'll go higher if I turn the burner on to heat the air inside the canopy, and when we land I'll open a vent to allow the air to escape from the balloon so that I can control the rate of descent.'

Jace was captivated by Eleanor's enthusiasm. 'I love ballooning because every flight is an adventure,' she told him. 'One day I hope to fly over the African plains. I've heard that the views of the wildlife on the Serengeti from a balloon are amazing.'

'And for an adrenalin junkie there is the added risk of landing next to an irate lion,' Jace said sardonically. When he'd met Eleanor fifteen months ago he had thought she was sweet and charming, but adventurous was not an adjective he would have used to describe her. 'What made you decide to train as a balloon pilot?'

'You did,' she said quietly.

He frowned. 'How so?'

'You made me feel like I was worthless. I needed to prove to myself that I deserved better than to be a pawn in your revenge.'

Jace swore. 'I never thought you were worthless.'

Eleanor turned away from him and curled her hands over the edges of the basket. 'Pappoús introduced me to ballooning. He had a friend who was a pilot and used to take me for flights.' Her voice cracked. 'I loved my grandfather and I foolishly fell in love with you. But you are as ruthless as you have told me Pappoús was.'

'*Theos!* I am nothing like Kostas.' Jace's nostrils flared as he sought to control his anger. But guilt curdled in his belly when he forced himself to scrutinise his behaviour. He had betrayed Eleanor's trust. Even worse, he had justified his actions by telling himself that in a war there were always innocent casualties. Hurting Eleanor's feelings had been the price he'd been prepared to pay to seize control of the Pangalos and destroy Kostas's legacy. Grimacing, Jace acknowledged that he could not change what he had done in the past. But he owed Eleanor his honesty before she married him.

The soundless flight of the balloon was surreal, and the air smelled crisp and clean when Jace inhaled deeply. There was something magical about drifting across the endless blue sky.

Freedom.

He remembered what it had felt like to be denied his freedom. Sometimes in his dreams he heard the sound of the warders' keys when the prisoners had been locked in the cells every evening. Each morning had begun with the cells being unlocked, surly men shuffling out into the corridors, the stench of sweat and the clang of metal doors.

'When I was younger, I spent two years in prison,' he said abruptly.

Eleanor stared at him. 'What did you do?'

'I was found guilty of grievous assault.' Jace waited for her to make a comment, but her silence gave no clue to her thoughts. He continued tensely, 'It's true that I punched someone. But I acted to defend Takis when I saw that his assailant had a knife.'

'Was the Takis you tried to protect the same Takis Samaras who you sent to persuade me to sell the Pangalos?'

Jace nodded. 'We go back a long way, and we're as close as brothers.' He rubbed his hand around the back of his neck to ease the knot of tension. He did not know how he had expected Eleanor to react. She was clearly curious, and he wanted to unburden himself of the secret he had kept from her.

'When my father died, he left debts which my mother had to pay off. Although she had helped him run the hotel, she lacked any formal qualifications and could only get low paid work. I quit school to get a job so I could help to support us.'

'Iliana told me that you pretended to be older than your age so that foremen would take you on as a labourer,' Eleanor murmured.

'I met Takis on a building site. He was young like me, and had left home to escape his abusive father. We went out one night and were set on by a group of youths. Running away seemed our best option as we were outnumbered, but Takis tripped over. I went back for him and saw the knife, so I punched the guy who was about to use it.'

'I don't understand why you were sent to prison for trying to protect your friend.'

'The assailant fell backwards when I punched him and hit his head on the pavement. He was knocked unconscious and slipped into a coma.' Jace grimaced. 'I felt really bad about what I'd done. I hadn't meant to cause serious injury. But the young thug who had attacked Takis came from a wealthy family and his father paid witnesses to say that I had started the fight.'

'What about the knife? Surely it was evidence that you had acted in defence?'

'According to the witnesses' statements there was no knife. It was mine and Takis's word against theirs, and in court no one believed us.'

'So you went to prison.'

'Takis took care of my mother while I served my sentence, and some time later I heard that the guy I'd punched had made a full recovery. I shared my cell with a British man who was serving time for embezzlement. He taught me to speak English, so at least the two years were not completely wasted,' Jace said wryly. 'When I was released from prison I got a job with a building firm and fell for the boss's daughter.' He gave a cynical laugh. 'Katerina refused to marry me after I told her I'd been to prison.'

'Oh, Jace,' Eleanor said softly.

His eyes narrowed as he tried to gauge what was going on behind her serene face. Was she judging him? 'I have no way of proving that my version of what happened is the truth. Takis will back me up, of course, but I realise you might not believe me.'

'I believe you.' She shrugged. 'There's no reason for you to lie. You don't care what I think of you. Even if you had committed a crime and deserved to go to prison, it would not change my decision. I have no choice but to marry you to clear my brother's debts. What made you tell me?'

'Our wedding is likely to be of public interest in Greece, and it's possible a journalist might dig up the story. I wanted you to hear it from me first.'

Jace exhaled heavily. 'I admit that I with-held my real reason for asking you to marry me a year ago,' he said gruffly. Remorse tugged in his chest as he accepted that he had hurt her. She had wanted Prince Charming, but Jace knew he was just an ordinary man with flaws. He could never have lived up to Eleanor's expectations of a fairy tale romance, but now at least she understood that they both had something to gain from marrying.

'Let's agree to be honest with each other for the duration of our marriage,' he murmured. The woman he had met a year ago had been uncomplicated and he could not believe that Eleanor had secrets. Although finding out that she was a balloon pilot had been unexpected. Jace acknowledged that he had jumped to conclusions about her friend Nigel. 'Is there anything you want to tell me?'

'Like what?' She sounded oddly defensive and turned around to activate the burner so that their conversation could not continue over the noise of the flames.

When it was quiet again Jace said casually, 'Do you have any other extreme hobbies—

cage diving with sharks, perhaps?' Was it his imagination, or did she relax when she realised that he was teasing her?

'No, nothing like that. I don't have any secrets.' Eleanor's gaze slid away from him and he was certain she had lied.

At Jace's house in Thessaloniki, Eleanor was preparing for her wedding. 'There, that's the last one.' Her sister huffed out a breath. 'Your husband is going to curse when he has to undo all the tiny buttons down the back of your dress.' Lissa stepped to one side, leaving Eleanor's reflection in the mirror. 'I hate to say I told you so, but I knew you would look stunning in a dress that shows off your sexy figure.'

Eleanor forced a smile. She had to admit that the wedding dress her sister had picked out suited her curvy shape. Made of white silk overlaid with lace, the dress's low-cut neckline pushed her breasts high and emphasised her narrow waist and the contours of her hips before the skirt flared down to the floor. Intricate lace detailing on the back of the bodice hid her scar, and a row of pearl buttons ran from the base of her neck all the way down the dress.

In the rush to choose a dress and shoes, as well as pack up her life to move to Greece, she hadn't considered the problem of unfastening the buttons so that she could take the wedding gown off. Her sister's assumption that Jace would undress her made Eleanor feel sick with nerves.

She had denied she had any secrets, but if they spent their wedding night together he would discover her physical imperfection. Jace might be so appalled when he saw the scar on her back that perhaps he wouldn't stick around to find out she was a virgin. Memories of her first boyfriend's horrified reaction to her scar twisted the knot of tension in the pit of Eleanor's stomach even tighter.

'Hey, where have you gone?' Lissa asked softly. 'You're not supposed to look sad on the most romantic day of your life.'

'I...' Eleanor broke off. Part of her wanted to confide in her sister and explain that romance wasn't on the cards in her marriage. She had become much closer to Lissa recently, but the memory of the conversation she'd overheard when Jace had likened her sister to a beautiful peacock and *her* to a dull sparrow still rankled.

'You must wish that Mum and Dad were here,' Lissa murmured. 'It's a pity that Mark couldn't make it to the wedding, but hopefully he will get the help he needs at the rehabilitation clinic in Ireland.' She squeezed Eleanor's hand. 'I'm glad we've got each other.'

'So am I.' Eleanor blinked back tears, hating herself for her silly jealousy of her sister. 'You look lovely.' Lissa's bridesmaid's dress was cornflower-blue, the same colour as her eyes, and her pale blonde bob framed her striking features.

Lissa grinned. 'I hope the best man thinks so.'

'He is Jace's best friend, Takis Samaras.'

'Takis…what a hunk. I'm going to flirt shamelessly with him at the reception.' Lissa walked over to the dressing table and opened a box from which she carefully lifted out a bouquet of palest pink roses. 'From your fiancé,' she said as she gave the bouquet to Eleanor. 'We had better go. The car is waiting.'

The rosebuds were beginning to unfurl and

release their exquisite perfume. Eleanor swallowed the lump in her throat and reminded herself that Jace had sent her the bouquet for no other reason than he wanted to convince the guests, especially his mother, that their wedding was a love match.

But she must not forget that their marriage was a business deal. The previous day she had signed a prenuptial agreement which specified that the Pangalos Beach Resort would become a shared marital asset. In the event of a divorce, both parties would receive a fifty per cent share of the hotel. A second document stated that the entirety of Mark Buchanan's debt to Jace would be cancelled when Eleanor became Mrs Zagorakis.

Everyone was happy, or so it would appear. If the bride's heart felt as if it were breaking when she walked into the Town Hall where the groom was waiting, none of the guests who saw Eleanor's serene smile would have guessed.

Jace was standing with the mayor, who was to conduct the wedding ceremony. But Eleanor only saw the enigmatic man she was about to marry, and her pulse quickened when she recognised the gleam of desire in his eyes as he watched her approach him. Jace looked impossibly handsome in a navy-blue suit that screamed designer. The superbly tailored jacket emphasised the width of his shoulders and Eleanor's breath left her in a rush as she pictured his naked, muscular chest beneath his white silk shirt.

Trying to ignore the voice in her head that whispered, *If only this was real*, she stood beside Jace while the mayor spoke the words of the civil ceremony, which was much shorter than a traditional Greek church wedding. Before she could blink, it seemed, the mayor pronounced them husband and wife.

Eleanor stared down at the gold band Jace had slipped onto her finger and tensed at the realisation of what the wedding ring represented. She was legally bound to him for the next few months. She glanced over at his mother, who seemed to grow frailer every day. Iliana was smiling and clearly delighted to see her son finally married.

But then Jace lowered his head and every thought flew from Eleanor's mind when he brushed his lips across hers. There had barely been any physical contact between them since he'd kissed her on the night of the storm, more than a month ago. A few times his arm had brushed against hers when they had been walking next to each other and once, when she had been chatting to his mother, Jace had sat down on the sofa beside her and casually looped his arm around her shoulders. She had been excruciatingly aware of the hardness of his thigh pressed up against her.

Now Eleanor's heart pounded as he dipped his tongue into her mouth and the kiss became intensely sensual. Her senses went haywire when she smelled his spicy cologne and heard his low groan as her lips parted beneath his passionate onslaught. She clutched his jacket and felt the warmth of his body through the material. The taste of him lingered on her lips when he eventually lifted his head, and the predatory gleam in his dark eyes sent a quiver of longing through her.

But then he stepped away from her and she snatched her hand from his chest, her cheeks reddening when Jace said softly, 'I'm looking forward to being alone with you later, *omor-*

fiá mou, but first we have to get through the reception.'

A marquee in the garden at his house provided seating for the fifty guests, most of whom Eleanor had not met before. A few were business colleagues. Many of Jace's friends were entrepreneurs like him, successful men who worked and played hard. Some had glamorous wives and others, like Takis Samaras, were lone wolves who had no desire to settle down.

Jace had been the leader of the wolf pack, Eleanor surmised. During the wedding dinner she was aware that several women sent him overt or even quite blatant glances. The idea that the sophisticated socialites were his ex-mistresses, or they were candidates for the position, evoked a corrosive burn in the pit of her stomach which she assured herself was not jealousy. She discovered that drinking a glass of champagne made her feel less tense, and by her third, or possibly her fourth glass, she really didn't care if Jace had a different mistress for every day of the week.

When dusk fell the garden was illuminated by hundreds of fairy lights that danced in the faint breeze like golden fireflies. The air was filled with the scents of jasmine and orange blossom and fragrant roses that had been twined around the supporting pillars of the marquee.

The wedding was everything Eleanor had dreamed of when she had been in love with Jace, but it was all fake and she was suddenly tired of trying to keep up the pretence. Her jaw ached from smiling, she had a thumping headache and she was desperately thirsty. But when she beckoned to a waiter and reached for another glass of champagne from the tray, darkly tanned fingers closed around her wrist and pulled her hand down.

'I think you have had enough alcohol.' Jace's gravelly voice made Eleanor's stomach muscles tighten. He sent the waiter to bring her a glass of water. When they were alone she glared at him.

'Have you been keeping tabs on how much champagne I've drunk?'

'No, but I noticed you didn't eat much at dinner, and it's never a good idea to drink on an empty stomach.'

'You're not my keeper.' She hugged her

arms around her, fighting an urge to wrap them around his waist and rest her head on his big chest. Guests were starting to leave at the end of the reception and soon she and Jace would be alone. She felt vulnerable and out of her depth.

'I am your husband.' The possessiveness in his voice made her temper flare.

'That doesn't mean you can tell me how to live my life. Or were you planning to keep me barefoot and pregnant during our temporary marriage?' she asked sarcastically.

His eyes narrowed. 'If you *were* to conceive my baby, our marriage would not be temporary. I believe strongly that a child deserves to grow up with both its parents.'

Eleanor was startled by the intensity in his voice. 'Fortunately, there's not a chance that I'll fall pregnant by you,' she muttered, glad of the darkness that hid her hot cheeks as she thought of the contraceptive pills she'd been prescribed by her GP before she'd left Oxford. It wasn't that she planned to sleep with Jace, but it was better to be safe than sorry.

Eleanor heard her sister calling her name and was thankful for the excuse to hurry away from Jace. In truth, she did feel a bit light-headed and it was probably a good thing she hadn't drunk another glass of champagne, but she resented him treating her like a child. Inexplicably, tears stung her eyes. Her wedding day was over, and she was on her way up to bed on her own. She would have to ask Lissa to unbutton her dress with the excuse that she wanted to change into the sexy nightgown her sister had persuaded her to buy.

'I just wanted to say goodbye and good luck,' Lissa said when Eleanor met her on the terrace. 'I've managed to persuade Takis to give me a lift to the Pangalos. It turns out that he is staying at the hotel too.' She glanced over at the devilishly attractive man with jet-black hair and an unsmiling face. 'So far, he hasn't reacted to my subtle hints that I fancy him, but it's a two-hour drive to Sithonia and, fingers crossed, he'll stop playing hard to get.' She hugged Eleanor. 'I've got to go.'

'Just a minute…' Eleanor began, then sighed as she watched her sister scoot after Takis. She continued into the house and at the top of the stairs she walked along the corridor to the room she had been given when she'd arrived from England. It was connected to the master bedroom but the door between the rooms could be bolted from her side. Jace had said that for their marriage to be believable they must appear to sleep together.

Ten minutes later, her arms aching from reaching behind her back to try and undo the fiddly buttons on her dress, Eleanor conceded defeat. She spun round when the connecting door opened and Jace lounged in the doorway.

'I thought the door was locked,' she said in a breathless voice quite unlike her own. 'I usually check it, but I forgot tonight.'

'Perhaps one of the staff unlocked it. Or perhaps you left it unlocked on purpose,' he drawled.

'I assure you I didn't.'

He strolled further into her room. 'So you say, but your body is sending out a different message, *pouláki mou.*'

'*Don't* call me that. It's unflattering.'

'It's not meant to be.'

'You think I am a drab sparrow.' She took a step backwards and banged her hip on the corner of the dressing table.

Jace shook his head as he came closer. He had discarded his jacket and tie and the sleeves of his shirt were pushed up to his elbows. Wiry black chest hairs and an expanse of olive-tanned skin were visible where the top of his shirt was open. Eleanor hated how her heart leapt when his mouth curved upwards in a meltingly sexy smile.

'I think you are beautiful. When I saw you in your wedding dress you blew my mind,' he said gruffly.

'Stop right there.' Eleanor held out her hand to ward him off. She had been down this path once before, and she was determined not to fall for his husky voice and the seductive gleam in his dark eyes. 'You said you wouldn't force me to sleep with you.'

'Theé mou!' he exploded. 'Of course not. Do you really think that of me?' His jaw clenched. 'No, don't answer. I have a feeling I won't like your reply.'

He raked his hand through his hair. 'I wanted to thank you for marrying me and making my mother the happiest I can remember seeing her. She learned a few days ago that the treatment for her cancer has been unsuccessful, and there are no more options. It's simply a matter of time now.'

'I'm so sorry to hear that.' Eleanor bit her lip. 'But I feel terrible for lying to your mother, and my sister, and everyone who came to our wedding and wished us well, unaware that our marriage is a...a farce.'

'Is it?' Jace murmured. Somehow, he had moved without her realising and he was too close and yet not close enough.

'What else can it be?' she asked helplessly, mesmerised by his potent masculinity.

'Whatever we want it to be.' He slipped his hand beneath her chin and tilted her face. She felt as if she were drowning in his liquid gaze and her lips parted of their own volition when he brushed his mouth over hers in a featherlight caress. He kissed her again, taking little sips of her lips, tantalising, teasing. Not enough.

'This is not a lie. Our desire for each other is real and we are both enslaved by it,' he growled, his warm breath grazing her cheek before he kissed his way down her neck to the edge of her wedding dress.

CHAPTER SIX

JACE TURNED HER in his arms so that he was standing behind her and pushed her hair aside to gently nip her earlobe with his teeth, sending starbursts of sensation shooting through her. His chest rumbled as he made a sound somewhere between a laugh and a groan. 'That's a lot of buttons. I'll try to be patient while I undo them.'

His words chilled Eleanor's blood. If he unfastened her dress he would see her scar. His hands moved from her shoulders and she felt him release the top button. '*No.*' She was galvanised to action and jerked away from him. 'I don't want you…'

He stared at her and sounded puzzled rather than frustrated by her apparent change of heart. 'I would never do anything you did not want. But I know you want me, Eleanor.' His Greek accent was thick when he spoke her name.

She shook her head and the room whirled alarmingly. 'I don't... I don't feel very well.' Her stomach churned, and she gasped and fled into the en suite bathroom, just managing to turn the key in the lock before she leaned over the basin and was horribly sick.

When she'd finished and had brushed her teeth, Eleanor grimaced at her reflection in the mirror. Her face was as white as her wedding dress and her mascara was smudged, making her look like a panda. But she couldn't stay in the bathroom all night. As she stepped into the bedroom Jace came towards her carrying a glass of water and a plate.

'I had one of the staff bring you a sandwich.' He frowned when she shuddered. 'You need to eat something. How many glasses of champagne *did* you drink today?'

'I lost count,' she admitted. 'I didn't notice its effect while I was talking to the guests, but now I feel terrible.'

'I should have realised,' Jace said shortly. 'You are my wife and I am responsible for your welfare.'

His words sparked Eleanor's temper. 'I

don't want to be a responsibility. I'm not a child.'

'You act like one sometimes. Why did you run away in Paris instead of talking to me and having an adult discussion about what you had overheard me say on the phone?'

'You told Takis that your engagement to me was not a love match. What was there to discuss?' Hurt throbbed in her voice. She lifted her hand to her pounding head. 'Why is the room spinning?'

'You feel dizzy because too much alcohol in your blood can affect your balance. The best thing will be to go to bed, but you can't sleep in your dress. If you don't want me to take it off, I'll call a maid to come and help you.'

Eleanor was tempted to take the coward's way out. To delay the inevitable. She was sure that when Jace saw her scar his desire for her would cool rapidly from fiery hot to cold ashes. But perhaps it was better this way. He had said she was beautiful, but he would discover the truth and then they could continue with their marriage as planned—a business arrangement, nothing more.

'Let's get this over with,' she muttered, turning around so that she was facing the dressing table.

'I've had more encouraging invitations,' he said drily.

'I don't doubt it.' She remembered a stunning brunette at the wedding who had introduced herself as a member of Jace's finance team. Angeliki had made it clear she hoped for a more personal role in his life.

'Hold your hair up.' Jace's breath felt warm on her neck when she obeyed. She felt his fingers at the top of her dress as he worked on the buttons. Lower and lower he went, and now she was aware of the two sides of the bodice separating to reveal...

His breath hissed between his teeth. He did not say a word, but she saw his shocked expression in the mirror. Tears welled in Eleanor's eyes, but she forced herself to stand unmoving while he continued to open her dress down to her waist.

'Now you know,' she choked. 'I'm hideous.'

'No...'

'*Yes!*' She jerked away from him. 'You don't have to pretend that you're not horrified by my scar. I saw your face in the mirror. You think I'm repulsive.' Tears streamed down her face and her shoulders shook with the force of her sobs. This was the moment she had dreaded. Jace's shocked silence *hurt*.

'You can have any woman you want. Beautiful, perfect women with unblemished bodies. Why on earth would you want me?' She gulped air into her lungs. Her close-fitting wedding dress was constricting, and its beauty mocked her. 'Go away, Jace,' she whispered brokenly.

'I'm not going anywhere, *matia mou*.' Jace kept his voice unemotional, recognising that Eleanor's emotions were on a knife-edge. He could not deny he'd been shocked when he had uncovered her scar. But repulsed? Never. His insides twisted as he remembered the pain in her voice when she'd insisted that her scar made her ugly.

He had been rendered breathless by her loveliness at his first sight of her wearing her bridal gown. In the run up to the wedding he had been constantly aware of her. She had obviously followed his advice that she would need a new wardrobe for when they were married, although she'd refused to allow him to pay for her clothes. But seeing her in sexy outfits which showed off her fantastic figure had ratcheted up his desire.

The nights had been worse, knowing that she was in bed in the room adjoining his. Knowing too that the desire that made his body ache was mutual. Chemistry had simmered between them and his libido had been eagerly anticipating their wedding night.

Jace hadn't realised that Eleanor had drunk way too much champagne at the reception, and he guessed she was unused to drinking a lot of alcohol. He felt a tug in his chest as he stared at her tear-stained face. 'You can barely stand upright,' he said softly. 'Let's get you into bed. Where do you keep your nightwear?'

She pointed to a drawer and he opened it and pulled out a wisp of black silk. Colour stormed into her face when he held up the seductive negligee. 'Not that one, obviously,' she muttered.

'Why obviously?'

'A sexy nightdress won't change what I am.'

'And what do you think you are?'

'Disfigured. That's what a boyfriend called me when he saw my back.' She rubbed her hand across her face. 'Tony was in the sixth form at school. I'd fancied him for ages, and I couldn't believe it when he asked me out. We went on a couple of dates and he seemed to really like me.'

Her voice dropped so low that Jace had to strain to hear her. 'We went to a pool party at another friend's house. I felt nervous about wearing a bikini, but everyone was having fun in the pool...so I took my shirt off. When Tony saw my scar, he said it...it was disgusting. In front of all my friends he told me to put my shirt back on because my scar was repulsive.'

Jace swore. 'The guy was a crass idiot. I assume you broke off your relationship after he was so insensitive?'

'He dumped me right there at the party,' she said flatly. 'I felt so embarrassed. But he was right. My scar is an ugly disfigurement, which is why I keep it covered up.'

A red mist obliterated every thought in Jace's head as rage pumped through him and he clenched his fists. The one and only time he'd resorted to physical violence to defend his best friend had resulted in him being sent to prison. But he would willingly serve a life sentence if he could spend five minutes with the young punk who had cruelly destroyed Eleanor's self-confidence. Jace was taken aback by a feeling of protectiveness that he had never experienced before.

'You wore a high-neck swimming costume on the cruise around the northern islands.' He remembered she had looked wistfully at some colourful bikinis in a street market on Lemnos, but she'd refused his offer to buy one for her.

She nodded. 'I was flattered by your attention. You made me feel attractive, but I was afraid you would be put off by my scar.'

It was little wonder that Eleanor had fled from his hotel room in Paris after she'd overheard him tell Takis why he had asked her to be his wife, Jace acknowledged grimly. She had already suffered with low self-esteem and his behaviour must have felt like a betrayal. Guilt left a bitter taste in his mouth. He looked away from her vulnerable expression and took an oversized tee shirt out of the drawer.

She held out her hand for the shirt. 'Will you please turn around?'

Jace forbore from mentioning that he had seen her naked breasts before. He crossed the room and drew back the bedcovers, ready for Eleanor to climb into bed. She groaned as she lay back against the pillows.

He turned the lamp's dimmer switch to its lowest setting and pulled a chair closer to the bed before he sat down and stretched his long legs out in front of him. 'How did you get your scar—some kind of accident?' he asked gently.

She let out her breath slowly. 'I had a medical condition called scoliosis. Basically it's a twist in the spine which causes the back and shoulders to be misaligned. I was eight when it was first noticed that I was standing awkwardly. Mum was always telling me not to slouch. The GP sent me for an X-ray which showed that my spine was curved, and for the next five years I wore a back brace for twenty-three hours a day.

'That sounds grim. It must have affected your childhood.'

'I couldn't do many of the activities that my brother and sister were able to do.' Eleanor sighed. 'My parents struggled to cope with my condition. Dad was a famous show jumper and Mum had been a junior gymnast champion before she became a model. They had a glamorous lifestyle and I guess they were unprepared for having a child with a disability. When I was thirteen I had surgery to straighten my spine. The operation happened a few months after my parents died and they never knew that I was finally free of the body brace.'

The sadness in her voice twisted Jace's insides. Eleanor's childhood had been as tough as his own, albeit for different reasons. He had blamed Kostas for destroying his family, and still blamed him, Jace reminded himself.

The feud between his father and Kostas Pangalos had happened a long time ago. Of course he wanted to avenge his father's death, but he regretted hurting Eleanor. He wished he could turn the clock back, and that the situation between them was different. Jace frowned. What was he thinking? He had shunned long-term relationships and commitment for most of his adult life. Oh, he'd soon got over Katerina. But he had decided that love—the lasting kind—wasn't for him.

Eleanor's breathing slowed as she fell asleep and her long lashes fanned on her cheeks. How had he thought she was uncomplicated? Jace thought ruefully. She was compassionate, courageous, irritatingly independent, and she fascinated him more than any woman ever had.

The truth was that he should ignore his hunger for her and keep their marriage to a business arrangement as he had originally planned. Except that his plan had been hijacked by his sexy wife. She rolled onto her side and tucked her hand beneath her cheek. Her lips were slightly parted, and he longed to kiss her. But he was not her prince, he reminded himself. He could not offer her the happy ever after he suspected she wanted. Eleanor was a beguiling mix of innocence and sensuality and Jace had no idea what he was going to do about her.

* * *

Eleanor leaned back in the plush leather seat on Jace's private jet as the plane accelerated down the runway and lifted off the ground. She noticed that his fingers gripped the armrests at the moment of take-off.

'Are you feeling any better?' he asked her a few minutes later.

'I feel fine, thank you.'

'You're a terrible liar.' He sounded amused, almost indulgent, and she steeled her heart against his charisma. She winced when he removed the enormous pair of sunglasses that she'd worn to hide the evidence of her first, and she vowed last, hangover.

'The stewardess will bring some food, and after you have eaten you can sleep off your headache.' His smile did strange things to her insides. 'Aren't you curious to know where we are going for our honeymoon?'

'I don't care,' she said stubbornly. 'The only reason you sprung a honeymoon on me is to make your mother believe that our marriage is real.' She snatched her sunglasses back and shoved them on her nose. 'Anyway, I expect you would prefer to be jetting off with your attractive financial advisor. At the wedding reception, Angeliki dropped hints that you are interested in more than her numeracy skills.'

His soft laughter was like golden honey sliding over her, and for some reason Eleanor felt the ache of tears behind her eyelids. 'There's no need to be jealous, *pouláki mou*,' he drawled. 'It's a rule of mine not to mix business with pleasure and I am never tempted to cross the line between employer and staff.'

'I'm not jealous,' Eleanor snapped, thinking that Jace had not actually denied he was attracted to Angeliki. But, before she could press him further, the stewardess arrived and handed her a glass of orange juice. She drank it thirstily and managed to eat a couple of mouthfuls of croissant to satisfy Jace. She settled back in the seat, but her eyes flew open when a pair of strong arms scooped her up and held her against his chest.

'You will be more comfortable in bed,' Jace assured her, carrying her as if she weighed no more than a doll. He strode into the bedroom at the back of the plane. 'We'll be in the air for approximately eight hours. Perhaps you will be in a better mood when you wake up.'

'Why did you spend last night in my room?' She had been shocked to find him sprawled on the chair beside her bed in the morning.

'I stayed in case you were sick again, or needed anything. I don't think you have been drunk very often.'

'It was my first time.' She flushed, thinking of the other first time that she'd thought might happen on her wedding night. Maybe she was destined to remain a virgin for ever.

Jace sat on the edge of the bed and smoothed her hair back from her face. Apart from the thicker stubble on his jaw where his beard needed a trim, he was his usual urbane self and devastatingly sexy in pale jeans, cream polo shirt and a casual mid-blue blazer.

'Would you like me to stay with you now?' he murmured.

Her eyes locked with his and it would be so easy to melt in the heat of his gaze. The mysterious alchemy that was always there between them sizzled and she was intensely aware of him, and of her body's reaction to him. Her nipples felt hot and tight beneath her bra, and molten heat pooled between her legs when she imagined him stretching out on the bed and lifting her skirt up to her thighs so that he could slip his hand inside her knickers.

Eleanor swallowed audibly and Jace's eyes glittered when her tongue darted across her lower lip. It would be so easy to become spellbound by his magic. But afterwards what would become of her?

'No, that won't be necessary,' she said stiffly and shut her eyes before she succumbed to the temptation that was always and only Jace. She heard him sigh softly and seconds later the click of the door closing. Only then did she allow her tears to slide silently down her face.

It was dark when they landed and immediately transferred to a four-by-four that whisked them away to an unknown destination. Eleanor's headache had developed into a migraine and she barely noticed her surroundings. She was vaguely aware of Jace carrying her and laying her down on a soft bed.

'These are painkillers.' He gave her two tablets and held a glass of water to her lips. 'You must eat something, *matia mou*.' His voice was soft and low as if he knew that her head felt as if it might explode. 'Take a bite of this,' he urged.

She bit into a banana, swallowed and took another bite before she sank back on the pillows and into oblivion.

When she opened her eyes she had no idea how long she had been asleep, or where she was. Feeling disorientated, she cautiously sat up and was relieved that she no longer felt as if someone was drilling into her skull. In the shadowy half-light she made out the time on her watch. Five-thirty a.m. Her stomach growled. Wherever she was, she hoped they served breakfast early. She wondered where Jace was sleeping.

The silence was profound, but gradually she began to hear noises. Birdsong, but no birds that she recognised, and other unfamiliar sounds. And then it came. A deep growl that reverberated in the air and through her body. Primitive, awe-inspiring.

A door opened and Jace stepped into the room. 'Good, you're awake.'

'Th-that was a *lion*,' Eleanor stammered. 'Where *are* we?'

'Africa. Tanzania, to be precise, in the Serengeti National Park. How is your headache?'

'Gone.' She stared at him. He looked more gorgeous than ever in khaki chinos and a collarless white shirt. She was conscious that her hair was a tangled mess. 'Jace…?'

'You've got ten minutes to shower and get dressed before breakfast. We need to make an early start.'

'Where are we going?'

'You'll see.' His grin sent her heart into a tailspin. This was the Jace she had fallen in love with—which made him dangerous.

Half an hour later they were in the four-by-four, driving across the open plains. The sky had lightened to indigo and the sun was a band of gold on the horizon, against which broad acacia trees were silhouetted. Eleanor caught her breath when she saw a hot-air balloon being inflated by a couple of ground crew.

'There's our transport,' Jace said as he helped her out of the vehicle. The gossamer curtain of an early morning mist was beginning to clear and the dawn was almost upon them.

'This isn't real, is it?' Eleanor whispered. 'I'm going to wake up and find it's a dream.'

He gave an odd crooked smile, as if he felt pleased by her reaction. 'We have a pilot who is also a guide to tell us about the wildlife we'll hopefully see today. But another time you will be able to fly the balloon yourself, once the balloon company have checked that your pilot's licence is valid.'

Eleanor climbed into the basket and watched Jace do the same. 'But you dislike heights. You don't have to come on the flight if you would rather not.'

'I'm not letting you go up without me, *pouláki mou.*'

She told herself not to read anything into the possessiveness in his voice. Jace was a typical Greek male, she thought ruefully. She swallowed, trying, and failing, to control her emotions. 'Why did you arrange such a wonderful surprise?'

He exhaled deeply. 'I suppose I am trying to make amends.' At her puzzled look, he continued. 'From the age of fifteen my life was dominated by my hatred of your grandfather and everything Kostas represented, including his family.'

'Me, in other words,' Eleanor said flatly.

His jaw clenched. 'I wanted revenge for my father's death, and I was determined to claim my family's share of the Pangalos. I didn't care who I damaged along the way to achieving my goal.'

'I understand. I do,' she insisted when he frowned. It didn't make it hurt any less, but she accepted that Jace had not acted with deliberate cruelty a year ago. 'You didn't think of me as a person. I was simply a pawn in your desire for vengeance.'

'That's not true.' He raked his hand through his hair. 'Even though you were the granddaughter of the man I despised, I found myself liking you. The connection between us was not part of some elaborate plan. And the attraction still exists now. You feel it the same as I do.'

She coloured. 'That's just sex.'

'I'd like it to be,' he said softly.

Eleanor was aware of her heart thudding painfully hard beneath her thin cotton shirt. 'What are you saying, Jace?'

He captured her hand in his strong fingers and rubbed his thumb over the pulse beating frantically in her wrist. 'I'd like to call a truce in our marriage for as long as it lasts. It would be pointless to deny that I want to make love to you when I'm turned on simply by looking at you,' he said huskily. 'I think you want me too, *ómorfi gynaíka mou.*'

The warmth blazing in Jace's eyes when he called her his beautiful wife evoked a spurt of happiness inside Eleanor, and her heart refused to listen to the words of caution in her head. Her gaze locked with his dark eyes as he lifted her hand up to his mouth and pressed his lips against the new wedding band on her finger.

'You're not wearing your engagement ring,' he commented.

'I'm scared I'll lose it. A diamond that size must be extremely valuable.'

'But you don't value things by their financial worth,' he said musingly.

Their conversation could not continue over the roar of the burner as the pilot prepared for take-off. The ground crew let go of the tether ropes and the balloon rose gracefully into the air. Eleanor saw Jace's knuckles whiten as he gripped the edge of the basket. He caught her gaze and his sheepish grin caused the bubble of happiness inside her to expand.

'Ballooning is recognised as the safest form of aviation,' she told him.

He gave her a sardonic look. 'We are standing in a picnic basket suspended beneath an oversized tablecloth, and the balloon is powered by a glorified Bunsen burner. What part of that is safe?'

'But look at the views.' She caught her breath. 'Look, down there…giraffes…do you see them? Oh, my goodness, there's a baby one.'

Their pilot and guide, Yaro, smiled. 'Plenty more animals for you to see. I'll fly low over the watering hole where there will be zebra and elephants. And we should spot some lions. The National Park has the biggest population of lions in Africa.'

Eleanor leaned back against Jace's chest when he slid his arms around her waist and drew her close. The air was cool in the early morning before the sun had properly risen, and she revelled in the warmth of his body and the hardness of his thighs pressed against her bottom.

Beneath them the majestic panorama of the Serengeti stretched as far as the eye could see. 'I think this must be the most beautiful sight on earth,' she whispered.

'I agree.' Jace's voice was very deep. Eleanor was unaware that he was looking at her when he spoke.

It had been a truly magical day, Eleanor thought later in the evening. After the balloon flight, their guide had driven them to a camp beside a lake and they'd eaten lunch while they watched a huge flock of flamingos wading through the shallows. The birds' bright pink feathers made a stunning contrast to the blue lake. In the afternoon they'd climbed into an open-roof truck and headed out across the plains, where they saw majestic elephants and dainty impala and, incredibly, a rare black rhino. Tears had filled Eleanor's eyes when they'd spotted a lioness with three cubs.

'Africa is everything I had imagined and so much more,' she'd whispered to Jace.

'I'm glad, *pouláki mou.*' His expression had been hidden behind his sunglasses but the warmth in his voice had curled around her heart. She had told herself not to read too much into the easy companionship she felt with him. He had suggested a truce but in the same breath he'd reminded her that their marriage was temporary.

Now they were back at their luxury lodge. Eleanor had washed off the dust from the day with a relaxing bubble bath while she'd watched the short but dramatic sunset through the window. The sky had turned into an artist's palette of purple, pink and gold as the huge orange sun sank below the horizon.

Dinner had been prepared and served in the lodge by friendly staff. She and Jace had sat on the terrace, eating delicious food and listening to the night-time sounds of the Serengeti—the trumpeting of elephants, hyenas howling and the repetitive chirring of the nightjars in competition with the frantic chirping of cicadas.

When the staff left and they were alone, Eleanor stood by the balcony rail and looked up at the inky-black sky, scattered with a million stars.

'The full moon looks close enough to touch,' she murmured when Jace strolled over to join her. Throughout the day she had been intensely aware of him when he'd sat beside her in the truck with his arm casually draped across her shoulders, or lightly touched her face to draw her attention to a herd of wildebeest in the distance.

She inhaled the spicy scent of his cologne mixed with something earthier and profoundly masculine, uniquely Jace. He had changed for dinner and his black trousers and matching shirt emphasised his tall, muscular physique. Liquid warmth pooled between her thighs, and she felt the sharp pinch of her nipples and did not need to look down to know that their outline was visible beneath her amber silk wrap dress. The material felt sensual against her breasts and the glitter in Jace's eyes during dinner had told her that he knew she wasn't wearing a bra.

Eleanor took a deep breath before she turned to face him. 'I've been thinking about what you said earlier, and… I agree.'

One black brow quirked. 'You agree with what, exactly?'

Her thoughts had gone round in circles all day and returned to the one thing she was certain of. She was attracted to Jace—fiercely, overwhelmingly attracted in a way she had never been with any other man. He had said he wanted to have sex with her, but he'd made no attempt to sell her a romantic ideal. Jace had been honest with her, and she was tired of playing games. But admitting in words what she wanted was daunting.

'This,' she murmured. She placed her hand on his chest and felt the uneven thud of his heart beneath her fingertips. Moving her hand higher, her fingers gripped the collar of his shirt and she lifted up on her toes and pressed her lips against his mouth.

His immediate response banished her fear that she might have read the situation wrong. With a low growl that sounded as predatory as the lions who roamed the plain, Jace seized her in his arms and pulled her against his whipcord body. For a few seconds he allowed her to take the lead, and she kissed him lingeringly, flicking her tongue out to explore the sensual shape of his lips.

He made a rough sound and took control, sliding one hand into her hair to clasp the back of her head as he deepened the kiss and it became spine-tinglingly erotic. He tasted of whisky and desire. She opened her mouth to the demanding pressure of his and traded kiss for kiss as their passion grew hotter, wilder, a conflagration that blazed out of control.

Jace lifted his head and stared down at her, and the stark hunger glinting from his narrowed gaze stoked Eleanor's excitement. But when he caught hold of her hand and drew her inside the lodge and into the master bedroom she halted in the doorway and looked at the enormous bed beneath a canopy.

'Wait.'

He released his breath slowly. 'Of course you can change your mind, *omorfiá mou,*' he said in a strained voice.

'I haven't, but *you* might when I tell you

that I haven't done this before.' She watched his face as comprehension dawned and he frowned when she whispered, 'You will be my first.'

CHAPTER SEVEN

'WHY ME?' JACE refused to acknowledge the inexplicable euphoria that swept through him following Eleanor's admission. It had crossed his mind once or twice that she might be a virgin, but he hadn't really believed it. If he had not known that she couldn't tell a lie convincingly to save her life, he would find it hard to believe her now.

He was a red-blooded male and she was all of his fantasies rolled into one in a silky dress that clung to her sweet curves. During dinner, he had been too distracted by picturing her naked breasts beneath her dress to do justice to the food. The outline of her pebble-hard nipples jutting through the silky material had kept him in a permanent state of arousal. But there were bigger issues at play here than his out of control libido.

'If you have chosen me to be your first lover because of a misguided belief that my emotions will be involved, I have to tell you that you'll be disappointed,' he said tautly.

'Why?' She threw his question back at him. 'Don't you believe in love?'

He shrugged. 'I believe it exists for some people, but more often it comes with unrealistic expectations.' Somewhere deep inside Jace was the teenage boy who had discovered his father's body. He was haunted by the unanswered question of whether Dimitri had chosen death and deliberately abandoned his family. Jace associated love with pain and loss. Who needed love? Not him.

Eleanor met his gaze steadily. 'If you are worried that I'll fall in love with you, don't be. I gave you my heart once and you trampled all over it. I won't offer it again.' She shrugged. 'But you are very attractive, and I've fancied you for ages. I'd like my first sexual experience to be with a man who knows what he is doing.'

Jace told himself he was relieved by her assurance, but he was stung by her cool tone. 'How come you are a virgin at twenty-five?'

The slight tremor of her lower lip betrayed her vulnerability and stirred his protective instincts. 'Tony, the boy from school, was my first boyfriend. His reaction to my scar knocked my confidence and I retreated from the dating scene and focused on getting good grades in my exams.'

Eleanor sighed. 'Pappoús was so proud when I was accepted into Oxford University. He made it clear that he did not want me to be distracted from my studies, so I didn't get involved much in student life because I wanted his approval. As a child with scoliosis I was sure that my parents couldn't love me as much as they loved my brother and sister, but when they died I was my grandfather's favourite. I realise now that he was controlling,' she said ruefully. 'He groomed me from when I was quite young to be his successor as head of Gilpin Leisure.'

Eleanor said earnestly, 'I'm not ruthless like Pappoús, and I regret that he cheated your father out of his share of the Pangalos.'

The protective feeling that Jace could not ignore tugged in his chest when he saw the sparkle of tears on her lashes. 'I knew within minutes of meeting you that you are not morally reprehensible like your grandfather,' he told her gruffly. He ran his finger lightly down her cheek, tracing the path of a single tear, and then walked across the room and switched on the music system.

'Dance with me,' he murmured when he returned to her and drew her into his arms.

'You want to *dance*?'

She was stiff with tension, her eyes huge and full of uncertainty. Her defencelessness made his gut twist because he knew he must accept some of the blame for her wariness. But there was awareness in her gaze too. Desire that he easily recognised because it burned in him with the same fierce intensity.

'Humour me, hmm?' He urged her to move with him to the slow tempo of the seductive jazz number, sliding his hand down to her bottom to pull her closer so that her pelvis was flush with his. He heard her soft gasp when she felt the hardness of his arousal. And he ached. *Theos,* how he ached to carry her over to the bed, shove her dress up to her waist and thrust his swollen shaft between her soft thighs.

But Jace knew he must curb his impatience. His beautiful virginal wife needed careful handling. His wife! Odd how possessive he felt, and in a far recess of his mind an alarm bell sounded. He ignored it and continued to dance with her, hip to hip, her soft breasts crushed against the hard wall of his chest. The sultry fragrance of her perfume filled his senses when he pressed his lips to her throat and kissed his way up to nuzzle the tender place behind her ear.

Gradually he felt her relax as their bodies swayed with the music. Eleanor rubbed her pelvis sinuously against him. *Don't rush her*, Jace warned himself, but he had never known desire like this, so hot and urgent. She entranced him more than any woman ever had, and he exhaled a ragged breath when he untied the front of her dress and pushed the two sides apart.

Her breasts were perfect round peaches, the creamy skin softly flushed with pink and tipped with darker nipples that swelled to hard peaks when he stroked his thumb pads over them. He pushed her dress off her shoulders so that she was naked apart from a pair of tiny panties. When he slipped his hand between her legs he felt the wetness of her arousal that drenched her silky underwear.

'Jace…' Eleanor's sweet breath filled his mouth and he felt a quiver run through her as he eased the panel of her knickers aside and rubbed his finger over her moist opening until, like a rosebud unfurling, her soft folds parted to allow him to push the tip of his finger into her.

For her—all for her. He fought to bring his rampant libido under control, but his resolve to take things slowly was tested when she undid his shirt buttons and skimmed her hands over his bare chest. With a muttered curse, he scooped her up in his arms and strode over to the bed. He laid her on the mattress and rolled her onto her stomach.

She instantly tensed and tried to turn over, but he gently held her there with a hand on her shoulder and traced his other hand lightly along her spine, following the path of the thin white scar that snaked all the way down from her neck to the small of her back. She flinched, and he instantly stopped.

'Does your scar hurt when I touch it?'

'No. But how can you bear to touch it?' she choked. 'It's grotesque.'

Jace frowned. 'Do you often take a look at your back?'

'I never look at it. The nurse in the hospital held up a mirror so that I could see my scar after she had removed the dressing. I was so shocked.' There was a catch in Eleanor's voice. 'The nurse warned me that there was still a lot of bruising, which would fade, but the scar looked like I had been sliced in half. It's an ugly, raised purple wound.' She pushed up from the mattress. 'Please don't look at it. I hate it. I hate…my body.'

'Eleanor, *mou*,' Jace said deeply. His lungs felt oddly constricted when she hung her head and refused to look at him. A tear dripped from her face onto the black satin bedsheet and was joined by another damp spot and another. He stood up and held out his hand to her. 'Come with me.'

'It's all right,' she whispered. 'I don't need you to escort me to my bedroom.'

She swung her legs off the bed, and he caught hold of her hand and led her over to the long mirror on the wall. 'Stand there.'

'Why? What are you doing?'

Instead of replying, Jace picked up the free-standing mirror from the dressing table and positioned himself behind her, holding the mirror at an angle so that Eleanor could see the reflection of her back. 'Your scar is not as you have pictured it in your mind,' he said softly. 'It's more than ten years since you had the surgery, and perhaps immediately afterwards the scar was more obvious. As you can see, it has faded. But, even if it hadn't, a scar would not detract from your beauty.'

He saw her throat work as she swallowed. 'It...it's not as bad as I thought,' she said slowly. 'Not as red and lumpy as it was in the hospital.' Her eyes met Jace's in the mirror. 'But I am scarred. My body will never be perfect.'

'Your body would not be *your* body without your scar,' he said intently. 'You are perfect. There is a quote by a philosopher, Matshona Dhliwayo: "*Scars are a warrior's beauty marks.*" You are a warrior, Eleanor.' Jace turned her to face him and wiped away her tears with his thumb pads. 'You are not defined by your scar, but your strength and great compassion are a result of everything you have been through.'

Eleanor was drowning in Jace's dark gaze. She did not feel like a warrior and her stomach gave a nervous flip when he moved his hand to the zip on his trousers. She watched him undress and caught her breath when he lowered his boxer shorts to reveal the jutting, hard length of his manhood. Naked, he was a Greek god: powerfully muscular, his bronzed skin gleaming like satin in the lamplight.

'If you keep looking at me like that, this is going to be over embarrassingly quickly,' he growled. 'I want to make your first time good for you.'

She bit her lip and dragged her gaze from his impressively large erection up to his face. 'I've never touched a man…there,' she admitted.

'*Theos!* You're going to kill me.' He took her hand and placed it on his body, where the dark hairs grew thickly at his groin. Eleanor was fascinated by his masculine form as she ran her fingers lightly along his shaft and he shuddered. He felt like steel wrapped in velvet and the prospect of taking him inside her made her hesitate.

'Are you sure you want to go ahead with this?' Jace asked thickly. 'I would not try to force you in any way.'

Eleanor remembered the accusation she had made on their wedding night and felt ashamed. 'I know you wouldn't,' she quickly assured him. 'But... I don't want you to have sex with me out of pity.'

'*Opa!*' Jace looked stunned for a moment. 'The only person I pity is me. I've been tied up in knots for weeks, months, wanting you.' A dull flush ran along his cheekbones. 'The truth is that I haven't had sex with anyone since before I met you at the Pangalos well over a year ago, and celibacy is not a state I particularly enjoy.'

She stared at him. 'But in Paris you didn't...'

'Make no mistake, I was looking forward to making love to you. After you left, having sent back your ring, I assumed I would forget about you. But you were on my mind a lot,' he muttered.

'I couldn't forget you either,' Eleanor whispered. The wound he had inflicted on her heart healed a little, knowing that he had desired her in Paris. Perhaps even the deepest scars faded in time. She curled her fingers around his erection and heard his swiftly indrawn breath. 'I know this isn't for ever, but right now I want to have sex with you.' She knew she was blushing, but she ploughed on. 'You said that you want to make love to me… so what are you waiting for?'

From across the Serengeti plains came the thunder roar of a lion. The primitive sound reverberated around the room. A male preparing to mate. Jace clamped his hand over Eleanor's. 'Touch me like this,' he commanded softly, sliding her hand up and down his penis in a rhythmic action.

'Like this?' She felt a thrill of feminine pleasure when he groaned.

'Exactly like that, *pouláki mou.*' His eyes glittered as he hooked his fingers into her knickers and tugged them down her legs. 'Allow me to return the pleasure.' He slipped his hand between her legs and rubbed his thumb pad across the tight nub of her clitoris, sending starbursts of exquisite sensation through her.

This time when he lifted her into his arms and carried her over to the bed, he laid her on her back and straddled her, his knees on either side of her hips. And then he leaned forwards and claimed her mouth in an intensely sensual kiss that plundered her soul. Time ceased to exist, and Eleanor was conscious only of Jace's lips trailing a path down her throat and lower.

Sitting back on his haunches, he cradled her breasts in his palms and his clever fingers played with her nipples before he bent his head and took one taut peak into his mouth. The feeling of him sucking, hard, drew a moan from her and she clutched his hair and held him to his task. He moved across to her other nipple and drew wet circles around it with his tongue, teasing her until she made a husky plea and he closed his lips around the sensitive tip.

When her whimpers told him that she could not take any more of the sweet torment he was inflicting on her breasts, he shifted so that he was stretched out beside her and feathered his hand over her skin, exploring the indent of her waist and her flat stomach. His fingers traced lazy patterns in the cluster of dark gold curls between her thighs before he pushed her legs apart and stroked her inner thigh.

She moved restlessly, wanting him to… Her breath left her in a rush when he slid a finger into her wet heat and stretched her a little so that he could insert a second finger.

'Jace…' She gasped his name and arched her hips towards his hand as sensation built when he swirled his fingers inside her. Ripples deep in her pelvis warned that she was close to climaxing. It was tempting to go with the insistent drumbeat in her veins, but instinctively she knew that the pleasure would be even greater when he possessed her fully. She pushed his hand away. 'I want…'

'I know, *matia mou.*' His voice was like rich velvet wrapping around her. He rolled away and opened the bedside drawer.

'I'm protected,' Eleanor whispered shyly when she saw the packet of condoms in his hand.

'Well, then.' His sexy smile stole her breath. But when he positioned himself over her and pushed her legs wider apart, the predatory gleam in his eyes caused her heart to miss a beat. Excitement mixed with faint apprehension made her tense as he lowered himself onto her so that his steel-hard erection pressed into her belly. 'Try to relax,' he murmured against her lips before he kissed her slowly, his breath filling her mouth, the evocative male scent of him swamping her senses so that there was only Jace.

She felt the tip of his manhood against her opening and her feminine instincts kicked in, dispelling any lingering doubts, and making her impatient to feel his hard length inside her. He slid his hands beneath her bottom and lifted her so that her pelvis was flush with his, and then he eased forwards and carefully thrust into her, claiming her inch by inch.

Sweat beaded his brow and Eleanor sensed the restraint he was imposing on himself. She had expected discomfort but there was none, just a glorious feeling of fullness as he drove deeper, withdrew, thrust again and withdrew until she caught his rhythm.

'Ah, Eleanor, *mou.*' He spoke to her in Greek, soft words telling her how beautiful she was, and how much he desired her. She felt the thunder of his heart and heard the hoarse sound of his breaths as he increased his pace. His face above her had an intent expression that warned her he was losing control.

Faster, harder, she followed his lead in an age-old dance, and could not tell where she ended and he began. They moved as one, soaring ever higher, and suddenly she was there. He held her at the edge for timeless seconds, and then he moved again, thrusting deep and sending her spinning into the vortex of an orgasm that drove the air from her lungs in a shuddering, sobbing breath.

He wasn't done, and drove into her with an urgency that clutched at her heart. This Jace was strong yet vulnerable—her man, her master. When he let out a savage groan and collapsed on top of her while his big body shuddered with the force of his release, Eleanor simply held him and pressed her mouth against his rough jaw, trailing her lips up to meet his in a lingering kiss.

A long time later he rolled off her and she felt the coolness of the air circulated by the fan above the bed, and a coolness emanating from him that she knew she did not imagine.

'That was incredible, *omorfiá mou.*' Jace propped himself up against the pillows and folded his arms behind his head. His sultry smile was that of a satisfied lover, but his eyes were guarded. 'The next few months promise to be an amazing ride.'

It was a test, Eleanor realised, and one she had no intention of failing. She slid across the mattress and stood up. He had reassured her that he found her beautiful despite her scar, but she did not quite have the confidence to turn her back on him while she was naked. She picked up his shirt from the floor and slipped it on.

Jace's eyes narrowed when she sauntered over to the door. 'Going somewhere?'

'I'll spend the rest of the night in my room. I'm a restless sleeper,' she explained, not entirely untruthfully when she remembered the nights she had tossed and turned in bed, missing him.

'I have a feeling that I'm going to be restless tonight too,' he said drily. 'It makes sense to be restless together, *pouláki mou.*' His killer smile almost cracked her resolve to be as cool as him.

She shrugged. 'You know where to find me if you get lonely in the night. By the way, sex with you exceeded my expectations.'

Restless wasn't the word. Eleanor was too wired to sleep and when she reached her room she continued into the en suite bathroom, discarded Jace's shirt and stepped into the shower cubicle. Memories of his powerful body pumping into her stirred her desire once more so that she lowered her hand to between her legs and touched herself the way he had done.

'I know a better way to satisfy your urges,' a familiar voice drawled.

Her eyes flew open and she felt her face burn when she discovered that Jace had entered the shower and was watching her pleasure herself. She hastily snatched her hand away, and his throaty laugh was rough with sexual hunger.

'Don't stop on my account. It's pretty evident how much you turn me on,' he muttered as her eyes widened at the sight of his jutting erection. 'You drive me crazy.' He pulled her up close to his naked body. Rivulets of water from the shower spray ran down him, plastering the whorls of black chest hairs against his torso. 'Just when I think I've figured you out, you surprise me again.'

She hadn't imagined that he had deliberately created an emotional distance between them, and perhaps it was not surprising after the rapture of their lovemaking, Eleanor thought. Jace was worried that she might overstep the boundaries he had put in place.

'You're gorgeous, but you are not irresistible,' she told him lightly. 'I won't lose my head or my heart over you.'

His eyes narrowed and she sensed he was frustrated because he could not read her thoughts. 'But you did lose your virginity to me,' he reminded her softly. 'I'm honoured, Eleanor.'

Why was she playing this game when what she really wanted was to be in his arms and in his bed? she asked herself as Jace lowered his head and covered her mouth with his in an achingly tender kiss that became increasingly erotic. He trailed kisses down her neck and over her breasts, paying homage to each nipple until she squirmed and rubbed her hips sinuously against his burgeoning arousal.

'Let me finish what you started,' he murmured, pushing her back against the shower wall and dropping to his knees in front of her. She made a choked sound, half protest, half plea when he clasped her hips with his big hands and pressed his face between her thighs.

He used his tongue with an artist's skill and licked his way inside her while she writhed against his mouth, her shock at his intimate caresses forgotten as pleasure swiftly built to a crescendo. It was too much to bear and her orgasm was sharp and intense, making her cry out as aftershocks ripped through her trembling body.

When Jace stood and lifted her into his arms, Eleanor felt boneless and her head lolled on his shoulder as he strode down the corridor to his bedroom. The closeness she felt with him, the connection she had always sensed between them was just sex, she told herself firmly. She was not going to fall in love with Jace again because it would end in heartache. He had reminded her that their marriage had a time limit and, when all was said and done, he'd married her to claim his family's share of the Pangalos hotel.

Eleanor was so incredibly responsive, was Jace's first thought in the hazy moments before he was fully awake. The previous night he had carried her out of the shower and, in his urgency to make love to her, they hadn't had time to grab towels and dry themselves. He had taken her back to his bed and tumbled them both down on the black satin sheets.

She had been as eager as him for sex. If he had not felt the fragile barrier of her womanhood the first time that he'd made love to her, he would find it hard to believe she had been a virgin. The shy young woman he had wooed in Oxford, a lifetime ago it seemed now, had turned into a siren and he could not resist her lure.

But he'd long suspected that Eleanor had suppressed her sensuality. Last night had been a revelation. She had been uninhibited when he'd lifted her on top of him and she'd straddled him, supporting her weight with her hands on his chest as she'd lowered herself onto his swollen length. He had played with her breasts while she rode him, shaking her dark blonde hair over her shoulders and leaning forwards so that he could take one pebble-hard nipple and then the other into his mouth.

He had come hard and fast and his groan of satiation had mingled with her cries of pleasure as they'd climaxed simultaneously. Jace had found himself oddly reluctant to withdraw from her. When he had finally rolled her off him she was already asleep, and he had succumbed not long after her.

Now he stretched and felt the delicious heaviness of muscles that had not been used for too long. He had a healthy enjoyment of sex but, on the few occasions that he'd invited a woman to dinner in the past year, his libido had been worryingly non-existent and he'd made an excuse and dropped his date home at the end of the evening.

Jace frowned when he discovered that he was alone, and wondered if Eleanor had returned to her room during the night. *Theos*, she could be infuriatingly independent. Obviously, he was relieved that she understood the rules of their marriage. He had been concerned that she might hope for more from their relationship than he was prepared to give.

He was sure his fascination with her would fade in a few months. When they divorced, Eleanor would be able to search for a man who would love her as she deserved to be loved. Of course, there was no danger that she would fall in love with *him,* after he had emotionally blackmailed her into marriage.

Guilt twisted in his gut as he thought of his original intention to seize complete control of the Pangalos from her. Just before the wedding, he had changed his mind and asked his lawyer to draw up a new prenuptial agreement, which Eleanor had signed. There was no way she would find out that he had planned to betray her a second time, he assured himself.

Unsettled by the heaviness that dropped like a lead weight into the pit of his stomach, he rolled onto his side just as she pushed the voile curtain aside and stepped into the room from the balcony. Jace's breath snagged in his throat and he had no explanation for the sensation of his heart being squeezed in a vice as he studied her lovely face. Her wide hazel eyes sparkled with excitement.

'Oh, good, you're awake. You have to come and see the most spectacular sight.'

'The sight I'm looking at right now is spectacular, *omorfiá mou*.' Hell, he sounded corny, Jace thought ruefully, but his beautiful wife blew him away.

Eleanor blushed. 'You are just trying to persuade me back into bed.'

'Guilty as charged. If I throw back the sheet, you'll understand why I want you to take off my shirt and get your naked little derrière over here pronto.'

She gave a husky laugh. 'I will. But first come outside; there's something I want to show you.'

With a deep sigh, he grabbed his robe and padded after her. The lodge overlooked a watering hole where a herd of elephants were gathered. Jace counted at least twelve adults and several babies. In the early morning sunshine, the close-up sight of the magnificent creatures was awe-inspiring.

'Aren't they wonderful?' Eleanor whispered. 'Our honeymoon in Africa is the most incredible experience.'

He loved her enthusiasm and her joy for life. Her smile did strange things to his heart rate. When their eyes met, he was aware of a connection that he did not understand and refused to acknowledge as anything more than white-hot sex.

'I can promise you another incredible experience,' he murmured as he tugged her by her hand back inside. There he removed his shirt from her delectable body and shrugged off his robe. He kissed her lips, her breasts, pushed her down on the bed and spread her legs so that he could put his mouth on her and taste her feminine sweetness. Her husky moans made him harder, hungrier, and he hooked her legs around his waist and entered her with a powerful thrust, over and over again, until she tensed beneath him and his control shattered and they tumbled together into the abyss.

CHAPTER EIGHT

'How does it feel to be back at the Pangalos?' Jace asked his mother. 'It has taken a long time, but finally our rightful share of the hotel has been returned to us.'

'It has changed a lot since Dimitri co-owned it with Kostas. The refurbished hotel is almost unrecognisable, and the clientele are very glamorous.' Iliana sighed. 'Kostas was the visionary in the business. Your father was happy to keep it as a small hotel for families, but the truth is that it did not make much profit. Now the Pangalos Beach Resort is regarded as the best five-star resort in northern Greece.'

'I am sure the hotel's reputation would have grown just as well if Bampás had remained in charge,' Jace said loyally. It was not the first time his mother had hinted that Dimitri had lacked the flair to run a successful business. His father had been a kindly man, but he'd been no match for Kostas's ruthlessness.

Jace exhaled heavily. He'd felt on edge since he and Eleanor had returned to Greece two days ago from their honeymoon in Africa that he had arranged at the last minute. It had been unlike him to act impulsively, but her vulnerability on their wedding night had made him feel guilty that he'd forced her into marrying him.

Could he say that he was any better than her grandfather? he asked himself grimly. His ultimate goal had been to take full control of the hotel. It had seemed so simple. Kostas had destroyed his father, and so he would destroy Kostas's legacy. But Jace had come to realise that he did not want to hurt Eleanor more than he already had. She had innocently been caught up in the feud between their families, but now they both owned fifty per cent of the Pangalos and it was time to forget about the past.

He frowned, thinking of how Eleanor had insisted that she wanted to live at the Pangalos resort rather than at his house in Thessaloniki.

'It makes sense for the manager of the hotel to live on the resort so that I can deal with any problems that arise immediately,' she'd argued. 'It's a couple of hour's drive to your office in Thessaloniki. I'm sure you will want to focus your attention mainly on Zagorakis Estates, so why don't you base yourself in the city during the week and spend the weekends at the Pangalos?'

'You are my wife,' he'd reminded her tersely. 'Our marriage will not seem convincing if we live apart most of the time.'

Jace told himself it was a good sign that Eleanor did not expect the honeymoon to continue now they were back in the real world. The two weeks they had spent in Africa had been great if he was honest. It was the first time since he had started his property development company a decade ago that his life had not been dominated by work. Sure, he'd allowed himself time to socialise, but every successful entrepreneur knew that more business deals were made through networking at parties than in the boardroom. He'd had mistresses, but he had never spent time with them away from the bedroom.

Eleanor had been a virgin until their marriage, but she'd proved to be a delightfully willing pupil and sex with her had left him feeling satisfied in a way he had never felt with his previous lovers. He'd assumed she enjoyed their lovemaking as much as he did, and he was rattled that she'd suggested they live apart. He was glad that she wasn't a clinging vine, but the Eleanor he had wooed sixteen months ago had been eager to please him, unlike now, when she was irritatingly independent and stubborn. But he had not really known her the first time he'd asked her to be his wife, Jace acknowledged. And having hurt her deeply once, he could not blame her for putting up barriers.

Jace was becoming familiar with the uncomfortable stab of his conscience where his wife was concerned. He forced his mind back to the present. 'Are you sure you don't want to come and live in the apartment here in the hotel which used to be our home?' he asked his mother.

She shook her head. 'I was happy living here with your father, but since he died there are too many sad memories.'

Through the window Jace could see the cliff that he had scrambled down when he'd heard his father's faint cry from far below. He'd cut his hands on the jagged rocks in his haste to reach the bottom of the cliff. The sight that had met him would be etched on his memory for ever. His father's body twisted at an unnatural angle, blood pouring from a wound on his head. Instinctively, Jace had known there was no time to get help. Dimitri's breaths had been laboured and he'd been barely conscious. But he had roused himself when Jace had knelt beside him.

'Promise me you will destroy Kostas as he destroyed our family. Take back the hotel any way you can for your mother's sake. It is too late...for me...'

'Jace?' His mother's voice pulled him from the dark place in his mind. 'Will you and Eleanor live in the apartment?'

'No,' he said abruptly. 'We have moved into one of the private villas by the beach. I thought that if you lived here, I would be nearby to take care of you.'

'Anna is a good nurse. And you will want to spend as much time as possible with your beautiful wife.' Iliana's eyes twinkled. 'Perhaps there will be good news before long. A baby,' she said when Jace looked puzzled.

'Ah! We are not planning anything like that at the moment,' he muttered, relieved that he had started to push his mother's wheelchair and she could not see his face.

'Don't leave trying for a family too long. I can't tell you how happy I am that you have settled down. Eleanor is the perfect wife for you.'

Jace pictured his wife when he'd left her asleep at the villa where they were now living. They had enjoyed each other twice last night, and he'd woken before dawn to find her pert derrière pressed up against his hip. The invitation had been irresistible, and he'd eased his erection between her thighs while he'd slid his hands around her to play with her breasts. The sex had been leisurely at first and then urgent as passion built to a crescendo and he'd climaxed seconds after her.

Give it a few weeks and his fascination with Eleanor would turn to boredom, Jace assured himself. No woman had ever held his interest for long. He helped his mother into the car and felt a pang when she leaned back against the seat and closed her eyes. The signs of her illness were evident on her lined face. He wished he had been able to bring her back to the hotel sooner. It was ironic that his mother seemed more pleased about his marriage than the fact that his name was now included on the deeds of the Pangalos.

The car drove away, taking Iliana and her nurse back to Thessaloniki. Jace hesitated on the steps of the hotel, tempted to return to the villa and Eleanor. When they were together he forgot about why he had married her. But that was a dangerous path to take. There was no future to their marriage, and he did not want there to be. He had decided a long time ago that he was better off alone.

He walked across the opulent lobby and opened the door into the office he had decided would be his. And stopped dead. Eleanor was sitting behind the desk—*his* desk. His eyes roamed over her scarlet jacket, which was buttoned low down and revealed a tantalising glimpse of the deep vee between her breasts. She seemed to have forgotten to wear a blouse, Jace noted furiously. It was something that Takis Samaras appeared to be well aware of, from the way he was staring at Eleanor's cleavage as he leaned over her, resting his hip against the desk.

His wife and his closest friend were laughing, their heads bent towards each other as they shared a private joke. Jace felt a sensation like corrosive acid fizzing in the pit of his stomach. He had never experienced jealousy before, but the sight of *his wife* smiling flirtatiously at another man made him want to rip Takis's head off.

Eleanor glanced over at him and Jace convinced himself it was a guilty blush that spread across her face. 'We have a visitor,' she said unnecessarily. 'Takis was telling me such a funny story.'

Jace gritted his teeth, aware that his friend could lay on the charm when he chose to. 'Was he?' he said curtly.

Takis straightened up and strolled across the room. Amusement gleamed in his eyes as he murmured, 'Good to see you, Jace. I thought I'd come and check out your new acquisition. The Pangalos,' he added drily when Jace's gaze flew to Eleanor. 'So, you finally took control of the hotel, as you always planned to do.'

After Takis had walked out of the office, saying that he wanted to take a look at the pool and spa, Eleanor glared at Jace. 'What's got into you? You've got an expression like you've been sucking on a lemon. I thought you would be pleased to see Takis.'

'Evidently you were pleased,' he said curtly. He raked a hand through his hair, perplexed by the wild emotions storming through him. He did not do emotions. But the possessiveness he felt for Eleanor made a mockery of his belief that he would find it easy to walk away from her when their marriage ended. The likelihood was that they would be able to divorce in a matter of months. His mother's health was failing, and when she was no longer here there would be no reason for him to continue with his fake marriage. Except that it had not felt fake when they had been on their honeymoon. He had enjoyed being with Eleanor, and not only in bed.

He forced his mind away from his confused thoughts when he realised that she was speaking.

'What did Takis mean when he congratulated you on taking control of the Pangalos? I agreed to give you a fifty per cent share. All decisions about the hotel will be made by both of us.'

Jace shrugged. 'I guess Takis made a slip of the tongue.' He watched Eleanor stand up and walk around the desk. His body clenched with desire as he ran his eyes over her slender legs beneath her short scarlet skirt. Her stiletto heel shoes made her legs seem even longer.

'I did not expect you to come to work today,' he murmured. 'Why don't you take a few days off to recover from jet-lag after the flight from Africa?' He stepped closer to her and slid his arm around her waist, drawing her up against him so that they were hip to hip. He knew she must feel the hard proof of his arousal. The pulse at the base of her throat was beating erratically. 'I have a few things to see to here and then I'll join you at the villa for a siesta.'

Eleanor pulled out of his arms. 'It's a tempting idea, but I have far too much to do. As you are aware, my brother left a lot of prob-

lems at the Pangalos that I need to sort out.'
She resumed her seat behind the desk. 'I
doubt I'll finish here until late this evening.
Maybe we can order take-out for dinner—
unless you want to cook tonight?'

In the past Jace had frequently cancelled a
date when work had demanded his time. But
he did not enjoy it when Eleanor made it clear
that she was prepared to prioritise business
over spending time with him. Once again,
he reminded himself that this was exactly
the kind of relationship he wanted. Eleanor
knew her own mind and did not assume he
would drop everything for her. The flip side
was that she would not change her schedule
because he'd asked her to.

What had happened to the lovestruck
woman who had been waiting eagerly on the
doorstep when he'd arrived to take her out to
dinner in Oxford? Jace brooded. The answer
struck him with a thud in his chest. Eleanor
had fallen out of love with him, and there was
no reason at all why the realisation made him
feel empty inside.

She glanced up from her computer screen.
'I put your briefcase in the smaller office next

door. No doubt you'll spread your time between the hotel and your business in Thessaloniki, so I might as well have the bigger office. There is one other thing I want to discuss with you.'

'Go on,' Jace drawled.

'Elias, who is head of marketing, told me that you had spoken to him about changing the name of the hotel to the Zagorakis. I disagree.'

'For what reason?'

'Changing the name will incur a lot of unnecessary expense at a time when the hotel's finances are unstable.'

'Due to your brother's mismanagement,' Jace said sardonically.

Eleanor flushed. 'True, and I accept some of the responsibility because I trusted Mark. But, whatever you think of my grandfather, he made the Pangalos what it is today, and you can't simply ignore the fact that it is his legacy. You are not the sole owner of the hotel. We own it jointly, and I won't accept changing the Pangalos to your name, Zagorakis.'

Jace's gaze narrowed on Eleanor's determined face. Did she have any idea how sexy she looked with her hair swept up in an elegant chignon and her full lips coated in a scarlet gloss that tempted him to walk around the desk and haul her into his arms? On one level he was annoyed that she was prepared to argue with him. He was used to getting his own way. But he found himself enjoying their verbal sparring. It was refreshing to have her challenge him and he admired her strong will, which matched his own. Being married to her would never be boring.

'Zagorakis is your name too,' he reminded her. 'My suggestion is to name the hotel after both of its owners.'

'Our marriage is a temporary arrangement,' she said coolly. 'I won't be Zagorakis after we divorce, and I'll revert to my maiden name.'

'Fine, we'll leave the idea of changing the name for now.' Jace did not accept defeat but he realised he would have to use different tactics to persuade Eleanor. His body tightened as he imagined employing various erotic methods of persuasion.

'Did the marketing director mention my other idea, to host a party here? Every year,

Zagorakis Estates organises a charity fund-raising ball which attracts interest from businesses and celebrities around the world. The invitations went out a few months ago, but we can notify guests of the change of venue. Apart from raising a lot of money for good causes, it will be good advertising for the hotel.'

'I think it is an excellent idea.' Eleanor's smile lit up her lovely face. Jace had no explanation for the way his heart seemed to expand to fill his chest.

Disconcerted by feelings that were new and frankly terrifying, he turned away from her and strode towards the door, growling, 'At least we agree on something.'

Butterflies swooped in Eleanor's stomach. At the last minute she was plagued with self-doubt. Why had she agreed to wear the dress to what was being labelled by the media as *the* party of the year? The charity fundraising ball had a guest list that read like the *Who's Who* of Europe's social elite, and a top magazine had donated a huge sum of money to the charitable fund established by Zagorakis Estates for excusive photograph rights of the party.

Eleanor's dress had been loaned to her by a famous design house. Made of ruby red silk overlaid with lace, the dramatic front of the bodice was eye-catching, but at the back the material skimmed her shoulders before falling away in a deep cowl to her waist and then fell in soft folds to the floor. It meant that her back was bare, and when she angled the dressing table mirror she could see that her scar was clearly visible.

She could not go through with it and wear the dress tonight, she decided frantically. The idea of making herself so vulnerable when people saw and perhaps commented on her scar made her feel sick.

Footsteps sounded on the marble floor outside in the hallway, and she whirled away from the mirror just in time as Jace opened the door and walked into the bedroom. He stopped in his tracks and stared at her, his expression unreadable as it so often was, but she noticed a nerve jump in his jaw.

'You look incredible,' he said in a rough voice that caused the tiny hairs on her body to stand on end. She reminded herself that he could not see her back. Jace had insisted that her scar did not make her unattractive, and when they were alone she almost believed him. But she wondered how he would react to the idea of her wearing a dress that drew attention to her naked back in public.

Her heartrate quickened when he prowled towards her. The feral gleam in his eyes evoked a wild hunger inside her and she felt her nipples harden.

'So do you.' She flushed when she realised that she had spoken her thoughts aloud. But it was the truth. He was breathtaking in a tuxedo that clung to his powerfully muscular body. This was only the second time she'd seen him in the past two weeks, and she'd missed him so much. Too much, a voice in her head warned. Since they had returned to Greece after their honeymoon, Jace had spent most of the time in Thessaloniki, while she had remained at the villa on the Pangalos resort.

He had told her that a problem had arisen at his property development company and he'd needed to be at Zagorakis Estates' offices in the city. There was no reason why he would lie, but she sensed that he had been deliberately avoiding her. The close bond she had felt with him in Africa had disappeared. Perhaps she'd imagined it had existed.

On their first day working at the Pangalos together, Jace had been different. Maybe he had thought she would hand the running of the hotel over to him. It would be easy to be overwhelmed by his commanding personality, but Eleanor had refused to allow him to dominate her. They owned the hotel jointly and she was determined to be involved in every policy decision.

'The guests will start to arrive soon, and as we are the hosts of the party we should be in the ballroom to greet them,' he murmured. 'Are you ready?'

She bit her lip. 'Give me a few minutes to change my dress.'

'Why on earth do you want to change it?' He reached into his jacket and withdrew a slim velvet box. 'The other day I asked you the colour of the dress you would be wearing so that I could select jewellery to match,' he said as he lifted up a stunning ruby and diamond necklace. 'Turn around and I'll put it on you.'

Eleanor hesitated and then spun round. She heard Jace draw a sharp breath and knew he could see what she had seen in the mirror. Her scar was even more noticeable now she had gained a light suntan, and it was a stark white line running down her spine.

'The designer asked me to wear the dress because the huge press coverage of the party will be a promotional opportunity for the fashion house,' she explained, her voice a shaky whisper in the silence, which stretched her nerves to breaking point. 'I… I agreed if they would donate money to the Scoliosis Support charity. It's a fantastic chance to bring public attention to the charity.' She swallowed. 'But now I'm not sure I can go through with it.'

Jace was so close behind her that she felt his warm breath stir the tendrils of hair that had escaped from her chignon and curled at her nape.

'I think it is a wonderful thing for you to do, *pouláki mou*.'

The gentleness in his voice brought tears

to Eleanor's eyes. 'You are the only person who has ever seen my scar, other than my first boyfriend when I was a teenager. What if other people have the same reaction as he did?'

'In that case they would not be worthy to breathe the same air as you,' Jace said fiercely. He sounded so protective, and her heart gave a jolt when she looked at their reflections in the mirror and saw admiration and something hotly possessive in his expression. This was the Jace who had made love to her on their honeymoon with a tender passion that had made her think he cared for her a little.

She gasped as he bent his head and pressed his mouth to her neck. He trailed his lips lower, following the line of her scar and restoring her confidence with each gentle kiss.

Lower and lower. Jace dropped onto his knees and continued his featherlight kisses down to where the scar ended at the base of her spine. With each kiss, the hurt and shame that Eleanor had felt at her first boyfriend's reaction to her scar eased. She felt healed inside, just as her skin had healed on the outside and was not the raised, angry scar that had so appalled her when she had been a teenager. Now the scar was a thin white line. It was not pretty but, thanks to Jace, she felt proud that she bore the mark of a survivor.

His hands were on her hips and heat bloomed inside. Desire for him, only and always him. When he stood up, she leaned back against his chest while he nuzzled the sensitive place behind her ear.

'You are beautiful, Eleanor, *mou*.' He sounded very Greek and his gravelly voice rumbled through her. 'But your beauty is not only skin-deep. You are beautiful in here—' he rested his hand just beneath her breast '—in your heart. At the party I will be proud that you are my wife.'

He eased away from her and fastened the ruby necklace around her throat. The stones felt cool against her heated skin. She met his eyes in the mirror and saw the hunger she felt for him reflected in his glittering gaze.

'Tonight I will make love to you while you are wearing the necklace and nothing else,' he promised. His sexy smile stole her breath. 'Hold that thought, *omorfiá mou.*'

* * *

Jace searched the crowded ballroom for Eleanor. One of the advantages of being so tall was that he could see above most people's heads. He spotted her standing by a pillar, talking to her sister. Anticipation ran as hot as wildfire through him. The party would end at midnight. He checked his watch. Twenty minutes to go. Somehow, he would have to curb his impatience to take his wife home to bed for a little while longer.

She had been amazing tonight, and no one but him would have guessed that she'd felt nervous about wearing a dress that revealed her scoliosis scar. It had been Eleanor's idea to pose for a photographer who had taken pictures of the backless dress. She had spoken honestly about the spinal condition she'd suffered from as a child, and the surgery to insert a titanium rod into her back, which had straightened her spine but left her with a forty-centimetre scar.

'I hope that by telling my story and showing my scar, I can encourage other people who have suffered the trauma of major surgery to feel proud of their scars,' Eleanor had told a journalist. She had looked at Jace and they'd shared a conspiratorial smile when she'd said, 'Scars are the badges of a warrior.'

Emotions that he could no longer deny swirled inside Jace. He had kept away from Eleanor since they had returned from Africa, believing that her impact on him would fade if he did not see her or have sex with her. Work issues at Zagorakis Estates had given him a convenient excuse to remain in Thessaloniki, but he had found himself thinking about her all the time, and many nights he'd almost given into the temptation to leap into his car and drive to the villa at the Pangalos resort to claim his wife.

Their separation had not lessened his desire for her, and this weekend he'd moved back to the villa permanently, or at least until his marriage ended, Jace reminded himself, aware of an odd hollow feeling in his gut.

'May I have the pleasure of this dance, Mrs Zagorakis?' he murmured when he strode over to Eleanor and slipped his arm around her waist.

Her smile was like sunshine on a rainy day, and when he led her onto the dance floor and drew her close she fitted against him as if her body had been designed exclusively for his. Jace wondered if she could feel the urgent thud of his heart beneath her ear when she rested her head on his chest. The light from the glittering chandeliers above them brought out the myriad golden shades of her hair. *Theos*, he would write a sonnet next, he thought sardonically. But as they swayed together in time with the music, nothing existed but him and Eleanor, and Jace found himself wishing for things he'd told himself he would never want.

'How is your sister?' he murmured, more to break the dangerous spell that Eleanor was casting over him than any real interest in Lissa.'I don't know.' A tiny frown wrinkled Eleanor's brow. 'She asked if Takis had been invited to the party and looked disappointed when I explained that he'd had to cancel at the last minute. And come to think of it, Takis said he couldn't make it after I mentioned that Lissa was going to be here. But he is here. I'm sure I saw him standing by the bar. Do you think something is going on between them?'

Jace shrugged. 'Takis told me his plans changed suddenly and he was able to come tonight. But as to a romance between him and your sister, I'm not so sure. Takis is a lone wolf.'

'Like you?' Eleanor suggested softly.

'Mmm, but I'm not planning to spend tonight alone.' His wife's scarlet-glossed mouth was an irresistible temptation and he bent his head and kissed her, uncaring that they were in public.

Eleanor was tying him in knots, but Jace could not forget that her grandfather had ruined his father. Guilt twisted like a serpent inside him. His unexpected feelings for his wife felt like a terrible betrayal of his father and the suffering his parents had endured after Kostas had seized control of the Pangalos.

There had been a time when Jace had planned to avenge Dimitri's death by taking the hotel from Eleanor. But he was shocked to realise that he did not care about the hotel or the feud. All he cared about was his wife's uninhibited response when he kissed her, and the gut-wrenching tenderness of her touch when she cupped his cheek in her hand and looked into his eyes with her clear and gentle gaze, as if she understood the confusion in his heart.

CHAPTER NINE

BRIGHT SUNSHINE REFLECTED off the white walls of the master bedroom in the private villa at the Pangalos Beach Resort. Beyond the open bi-fold doors, the azure infinity pool seemed to merge with the cerulean sea and the cloudless blue sky, while the vivid pink bougainvillea climbing over the trellis on the balcony was a sight to behold.

Eleanor sat up in bed and linked her arms around her knees. She loved early mornings before the hotel complex stirred, when the stretch of golden sand beyond the villa was empty of people and sun loungers. Summer was drawing to an end, but the weather was still warm and settled and the hotel was fully booked.

She and Jace lived partly at his house in Thessaloniki to be near his mother, and partly at the villa on Sithonia. Eleanor had fallen in love with Greece. Who was she kidding? She would be happy living anywhere with Jace, she thought ruefully when he strolled out of the shower room that he had made his own, while she preferred the en suite bathroom, which had a luxurious free-standing bath.

She had realised lately that she could very easily fall in love with her husband, who this morning looked mouth-watering in an impeccably tailored grey suit, crisp white shirt and navy-blue silk tie. It was little things that made inroads on her heart. Like how Jace always woke first in the mornings and brought her a cup of her favourite English tea. Sometimes, when she was in a rush to get to work, she would skip breakfast, but at her office she would find that he'd arranged for yoghurt, fruit and freshly baked rolls to be delivered from the hotel's kitchen.

He often bought her flowers and other little gifts: a book he knew she wanted to read, her favourite perfume, inexpensive jewellery when they wandered hand in hand around the market and she admired a necklace made of shells, or some pretty silver earrings. He gifted her with expensive jewellery too, and smiled ruefully when she preferred to wear a thin gold chain with an olive branch pendant that he had bought for her when they'd taken a boat trip to the island of Lemnos.

The trip had reminded Eleanor of when she had fallen in love with Jace on the island cruise, and she had warned herself not to rush headlong into repeating the mistakes of the past. But the olive branch necklace seemed like a symbol of hope. She returned the kind gestures Jace showed her by cooking meals that she knew he liked, and she made sure there was always a bottle of the single malt whisky he favoured in the cupboard.

Their relationship was not the sterile marriage deal that Jace had offered her, a lifetime ago, it seemed. He took care of her, and Eleanor could not deny that it felt wonderful knowing she could rely on him after she had spent so many years feeling alone and rather abandoned by her parents, who had not known how to cope when she was diagnosed with scoliosis.

As for her scar, she barely gave it any thought now, and she felt confident wearing a bikini or dresses with a low-cut back. On the night of the charity ball, Jace had told her she was beautiful and he had made her believe in herself. Never again would she allow herself to be defined by her scar. She was a warrior, and she would always be grateful to Jace for showing her how strong she was.

But dare she offer him her heart again? She knew him better now, and the truth was that she *liked* him. He was an honourable man who had been trapped by the promise he had made his father when he was a teenager to seek revenge after Kostas had destroyed his family.

Eleanor sighed. What she felt for Jace was not the infatuation she'd felt when he had swept her off her feet last year. With hindsight, she understood that he had been a fantasy figure—Prince Charming to her Cinderella. She had wanted him to rescue her from her dull life and her insecurities. But his betrayal had made her take a good look at herself.

She had realised that she'd been in awe of her grandfather when she was growing up, and always anxious to please him. And she had been in awe of Jace the first time he had asked her to marry him. She'd put him on a pedestal, but her expectations had been unrealistic. Now she knew he was a man with great strengths but also flaws that made him endearingly human and offered the tantalising idea that maybe he was not as emotionless as he wanted her to believe.

From outside the villa came the sound of a helicopter. Eleanor met Jace's dark gaze and something intangible and ephemeral hovered in the air between them before he gave a slight shake of his head, as if he found his thoughts puzzling. 'There's Sotiri to take me to the airport,' he murmured. 'I can't say I'm looking forward to the long-haul flight to Perth.'

'I know you said that the distance is too far for your private jet to make without refuelling, but travelling first class on a commercial plane means you will have a bed and you can sleep during the flight.'

'Mmm, I should get more sleep than I do sharing a bed with you.'

'Whose fault is that?' She pretended to pout.

He grinned. 'Yours, but I'm not complaining. I love your uninhibited response when we have sex.'

Love. Eleanor looked away from his impossibly handsome face, hoping he could not tell that her heart had leapt when he'd casually dropped the word into the conversation. How was she here again? she wondered. What had happened to her confident belief that she understood the difference between lust and love?

Was she a fool to think that perhaps there was no difference? When Jace made love to her it felt like more than just sex, although she did not have the experience to know if there was a difference, she acknowledged ruefully. Jace was the only man she had ever wanted, and a little voice in her head whispered that he was the only man she would ever want.

He had hurt her badly in the past, and the idea of laying herself open to being hurt again was terrifying. But sometimes in life you had to take risks. She was different from the person she had been when she had first met him. She was stronger and more confident, but was she brave enough to risk Jace's rejection a second time?

'Hey, where have you gone, *pouláki mou*?' The mattress dipped as he sat on the bed and slid his hand beneath her chin, tilting her face up to his. 'You have looked pale for a few days.' His voice was concerned when he brushed his fingers lightly against her cheeks. 'There are shadows beneath your eyes. Perhaps you are unwell. I'll call my doctor and ask him to visit you for a consultation.'

There were times like now, when Jace treated her with such tenderness, that made her think he might care for her a little. But she was afraid to hope in case the castle of dreams she had built came tumbling down.

She smiled. 'I don't need to see a doctor. You're not the only one who needs to catch up on sleep.'

He did not look convinced. 'Don't do too much while I'm away. I wish you had agreed to come to Australia with me. We could have had a few days holiday after I'd wrapped up my business meetings.'

'I thought I should stay behind so that I can visit Iliana while you are away.' Jace's mother had recently moved into a hospice. The doctors had said that she was unlikely to live to see Christmas, but mercifully she was not in pain and kept in remarkably good spirits.

Jace stood up, but he remained standing by the bed and stared down at Eleanor. His expression was hidden beneath his hooded eyelids. 'I'll insist that you come along on my next business trip.'

She nodded, but inside she felt sick at the thought that she might not be his wife for much longer. He had secured his half-share of the Pangalos, and when his mother was no longer here there would be no reason for their marriage to continue.

He leaned down and claimed her mouth in a lingering kiss that tempted her to pull him down onto the bed so that they could make love one last time before he left for his trip to the other side of the world. But she resisted because she did not want him to think she was needy.

'Bye then,' she said airily.

His gaze narrowed. 'Will you miss me?'

'I doubt I'll have time while I'm busy running the hotel.'

'Speaking of which, my lawyer has some paperwork for you to sign. It's to do with the planning application for the new villas we are hoping to build on the holiday complex.'

Jace picked up his briefcase and walked out of the bedroom without a backward glance. Minutes later Eleanor heard the helicopter take off. She dashed her hand over her eyes, angry with herself because she missed him already. It was the first time they had been apart since he had moved back to the villa, but she had better start getting used to living without him, she thought.

She had a job to do, managing the hotel, but when she got out of bed she was overcome by a wave of dizziness. It was not the first time it had happened and, although she had assured Jace that she wasn't ill, she did not feel right. There was nothing she could put her finger on but maybe she was slightly anaemic, which might explain why her period was a few days late.

In the bathroom she searched through the cupboard for the packet of multi-vitamins she'd bought the previous winter in England. It wouldn't hurt to start taking them again. Another box containing a popular herbal supplement that she'd used until recently fell onto the floor. She picked it up and happened to glance at the label.

Do not take if pregnant or taking the birth control Pill.

Frowning, she read the leaflet inside the box and discovered that the tablets could decrease the effectiveness of hormonal contraceptives. She hadn't mentioned to her GP when he'd prescribed the Pill that she used the over-the-counter herbal remedy which was reputed to help with mood swings. With a sense of dread she checked the calendar on her phone and realised that her period was ten days late.

She had been so absorbed in her life with Jace that she'd lost track of time. But she couldn't be pregnant, Eleanor reassured herself. Medications and even herbal remedies always came with a long list of contraindications, and the likelihood that the Pill hadn't worked properly was probably minuscule.

Over the next few days she tried to put the idea of pregnancy out of her mind, telling herself that she was worrying needlessly and her period was bound to start soon. But it didn't, and on the fifth day after Jace had gone to Australia, Eleanor drove to a village further along the coast to buy a test from a pharmacy. Few people at the Pangalos Beach Resort or the local area on Sithonia knew she was Kostas Pangalos's granddaughter, but everyone recognised her as Kyriá Zagorakis, wife of the wealthy new owner of the Pangalos. She did not want unfounded rumours that she was pregnant to circulate.

Early the next morning she stared disbelievingly at the blue line on the pregnancy test and checked the instructions again. *Positive*. Feeling numb, she sat on the edge of the bath, aware of her heart beating frantically in her chest like a trapped bird. Needless to say, this was not what she or Jace had planned to happen.

Jace! How would he react to the news? She was quite sure he did not want a baby. He did not want her to be his wife for any longer than was necessary to convince his mother that he had settled down to a life of domestic bliss.

He phoned mid-morning while she was at the office trying to concentrate on a financial report. It was some time in the evening in Perth, and he was about to go out to dinner with a business client. Jace sounded a million miles away and for once Eleanor was glad when he rang off at the end of their stilted conversation. She had decided not to give him her momentous news until he returned to Greece, although it was tempting to take the coward's way out and tell him over the phone rather than face to face. Her secret burned inside her, and she must have sounded odd because twice Jace asked how she was feeling.

Later that afternoon her secretary informed her that the lawyer had arrived. However, the man who entered the room was not the elderly lawyer Vangelis Stavridis, who Eleanor had met when she had signed a prenuptial agreement before her marriage. The young man who shook her hand introduced himself as Orestis Barkas, a junior member of Jace's legal team.

'There are a lot of documents regarding the planning application that require your signature,' he said, putting a large file on the desk. He rolled his eyes. 'Greek bureaucracy! Your husband has already checked the paperwork and signed it. I can see that you are busy and there is no need for you to read it all; just sign at the bottom of each page.'

Eleanor grimaced at the pile of papers, but her grandfather had taught her to read every detail before she signed her name and she picked up the first document. Some while later she was only halfway through the pile and heartily bored of the intricacies of building permits and energy performance regulations. The young lawyer was becoming fidgety.

'Seriously, you only need to skim through the pages. Jace is happy with everything.'

'I'm sure he is.' She had the odd sensation of hearing her blood thundering in her ears as she reread the typed paragraphs which stated that in the event of her divorce from Jace he would become the sole owner of the Pangalos Beach Resort. Eleanor would be unable to contest the agreement or change her mind once she had signed the document.

Somehow, she managed to hide her distress from the lawyer. 'Why don't you leave the paperwork with me and I'll have the documents couriered over to you when I've signed them?' she suggested.

'Are you feeling unwell?' her secretary asked when Eleanor stumbled through the door into the outer office a few minutes after Orestis Barkas had left.

'Actually, I'm not feeling too good.' It was the truth. There was a sharp pain beneath her breastbone where her heart had shattered and a dull ache in the pit of her stomach. 'I'll go back to the villa and try to sleep it off.'

She didn't cry. Couldn't. She was frozen inside and wandered aimlessly from room to room in the villa, ending up in the bedroom that she had shared with Jace for the past months. She pictured him sprawled on the bed, the sheet draped low over his hips and the bulge of his arousal a tantalising invitation. God, she loved the way he made love to her. He never made any secret of his desire for her and the possessive gleam in his eyes when he thrust his hard shaft deep inside her had given her hope that love could take root in even the stoniest heart.

But Jace's heart was a lump of granite. The damning document she'd found slipped in among the planning application paperwork was proof that he only wanted the hotel. Sure, he enjoyed taking her to bed, but he was unlikely to be pleased about the consequences of their passion.

Eleanor realised that she had not given any thought to the baby she was carrying. Her pregnancy seemed unreal, but in a little less than nine months she would have the responsibility of bringing up a child on her own.

Jace's name flashed on her phone and with a heavy heart she read his text.

It's midnight here and I'm about to go to bed. I wish you were with me, pouláki mou. When I come home we need to talk.

Indeed they did. She stepped outside onto the terrace and looked up at the stars that were starting to appear as dusk deepened to night. Tears blurred her vision and the starlight fractured as if she were looking into a kaleidoscope. Her phone pinged with another message from Jace, but she did not read it.

She had trusted him. Worse than that, she had fallen in love with him. There was no point denying it to herself any more. He had dismantled her barriers one by one and she had been powerless to resist him.

Fool. She had dared to hope that this time things would be different. But for Jace it had always been about the Pangalos and revenge. Fury swept white-hot through her and she lifted her arm and hurled the phone into the pool, watching it sink to the bottom before she collapsed onto the cold marble tiles and let her tears fall.

Eventually, when she was cried out, she knew she must go to bed and try to sleep for the baby's sake. But in the bathroom she discovered that there was no baby after all. The dull ache low in her stomach had intensified to a painful cramping and she was bleeding. An Internet search on her laptop revealed that early miscarriages were fairly common, and there was no need for her to call a doctor unless she bled heavily.

Eleanor felt bereft. It was no good telling herself that it was probably for the best. A baby would have been a link with Jace. She felt as if she were on an emotional rollercoaster. Jace's second betrayal was even more devastating than the first time he'd tried to trick her out of the Pangalos. The positive pregnancy test had been a shock. But now there was no baby and she had nothing.

Jace's business trip to Perth had been frenetic, and the long flight home had seemed endless. But he felt energised by the prospect of a shower, a stiff whisky and Eleanor beneath him. He reversed the order in his mind and smiled to himself as the helicopter prepared to land in the grounds of the villa.

He'd managed to cram a week's worth of meetings into six days so that he could catch an earlier flight back to Greece. The trip had been successful, and he'd finalised a number of deals that would ensure Zagorakis Estates' expansion into Australasia. But his mind was not on business as he pictured Eleanor's delight when he arrived home unexpectedly.

She never held anything back in her response to him, and his body tightened as he imagined kissing her soft mouth and cradling her gorgeous, pert breasts in his hands. Sometimes he wondered if he would ever have enough of her delectable body. But it wasn't just sex that he'd missed while they had been apart, he acknowledged. In the middle of important business meetings he'd found himself remembering how Eleanor's eyes lit up when she smiled, and the tender way she stroked the back of his neck when he lay lax on top of her in those mindless moments of utter relaxation after they'd made love.

Jace had also missed Eleanor's business acumen. They had become a team running the Pangalos, and more and more he respected her quick brain and her management skills, to the point that he was considering offering her a place on the board of his property development company. She had inherited her grandfather's instinct for recognising a brilliant deal and it was easy to see why Kostas Pangalos had made Eleanor his successor.

Jace frowned, unsettled by his train of thoughts. How had he allowed his relationship with his temporary wife to develop into friendship, a partnership and a closeness that had nothing to do with sex? Guilt snaked through him as he wondered what his father would have made of his marriage to Kostas's granddaughter. The two men had been bitter enemies and Jace had grown up hating Kostas. But he did not hate Eleanor. Far from it. He raked his hand through his hair and refused to examine in depth how he felt about her. She was his wife, and right now things were good between them, so why complicate the situation?

Dusk had fallen and Jace was surprised that there were no lights on in the villa. It occurred to him that Eleanor might be working late in her office at the hotel. But when he strode down the hall and saw a thin gleam beneath the bedroom door his heart gave a jolt which mocked his belief that he was in control of his emotions.

'Hey…' His voice trailed off. The spurt of pleasure he felt when he saw Eleanor quickly turned to confusion as he watched her walk from the wardrobe over to the bed and dump a pile of clothes into a suitcase.

She froze at the sound of his voice and gave him a startled glance before she turned her back on him. At the end of their honeymoon in Africa he had been amused watching her pack with military preciseness, but now she threw shoes and clothes randomly into the case.

'What do you think you're doing?' Jace asked her softly. He was aware of his heart beating painfully hard, and he felt the same sense of dread that he remembered feeling when he'd clambered down the cliff, following a trail of blood, and had seen his father's body lying in a twisted heap on the ground below.

'I'm leaving you.' Eleanor did not look at him, but Jace noticed that her hands shook as she rolled a silk blouse into a ball and shoved it into the suitcase. With an effort he dampened down his temper, sensing that her emotions were balanced on a knife-edge.

'Care to tell me why?'

'*Well, I wonder, Jace.*' She whirled round to face him, all semblance of cool gone, her eyes darkening from hazel to the sullen green of a stormy sea. 'Perhaps it has something to do with this.'

She snatched up a piece of paper from the bed and held it out to him. He took it from her, and his brows snapped together when he skimmed his eyes down the page. 'How did you get this?'

'It was tucked away amongst the paperwork

you sent your lawyer to get me to sign. Don't fake innocence,' she hissed when he shook his head. 'You are a lying, cheating bastard.' Her voice shook. 'Unluckily for you, Pappoús taught me never to trust anyone, even lawyers—especially lawyers.'

'Funny that, when it was Kostas's own corrupt lawyers who paved the way for him to cheat my father out of his rightful share of the Pangalos.' Jace exhaled heavily, remorse tugging on his conscience when Eleanor paled. 'I did not instruct Vangelis to ask you to sign this document.'

She gave him a disbelieving look. 'It wasn't Vangelis who came to see me. It was a younger man, Orestis… I've forgotten his other name.'

'Barkas. He recently joined my legal team, but after a mistake like this he can start looking for another job.'

'Don't shoot the messenger,' she said wryly. 'Whether or not the junior lawyer was meant to show me the document, the fact is that it exists, and you must have had it drawn up so that you could seize total ownership of the Pangalos.'

Eleanor shook her head. 'I was such a fool

to trust you for a second time. You keep telling me how terribly my grandfather behaved towards your father, but look in the mirror, Jace. You are no better than Kostas.'

His jaw clenched. But Jace could not refute Eleanor's accusation. 'I admit that immediately after you agreed to marry me in return for my promise to clear your brother's debts, I asked my lawyer to set out terms of our divorce which would give me one hundred per cent of the Pangalos. But by the time of the wedding I had got to know you better, and I instructed Vangelis to write a different prenuptial agreement giving both of us fifty per cent. That was what you signed before we married, and this—' he threw the document onto the bed '—should have been destroyed.'

Jace took a step towards her and cursed beneath his breath when she shrank away from him. '*Pouláki mou*, I am telling you the truth. I swear I did not attempt to cheat you out of your share of the Pangalos.'

She turned away from him and shoved more clothes into the suitcase. 'It doesn't matter. I don't care,' she said dully. 'This morning I did a pregnancy test. I'd been feeling weird for a while, and my period was late. The test was positive.'

There was a buzzing sound in Jace's ears. He heard Eleanor speak but the words that came out of her mouth did not make any sense. His shock rapidly turned to comprehension. No wonder she was behaving oddly, and her body was so tense that she looked as if she might snap. A million thoughts zoomed around in his head, but the question of how it had happened after she'd assured him that she was protected against pregnancy was not important.

'I told you on our wedding day that if you became pregnant our marriage would no longer be a temporary arrangement,' he said. 'A child needs and deserves to grow up with both its parents if possible.' Something fiercely possessive swept through Jace when he stared at his beautiful wife, and the mother of his child.

'Are you saying you would want to stay married to me if I had your baby?' Eleanor was clearly shocked. But the more Jace thought about it, the more he found himself liking the idea of making their relationship permanent.

'Absolutely. Divorce is now out of the question.'

'There isn't a baby,' she burst out. 'After the lawyer's visit I discovered that I was bleeding, and I'd miscarried.'

'Theé mou!' The tightness in Jace's chest felt as though his lungs were being crushed. 'Did it happen because you were upset after reading the original prenuptial agreement?'

'No, I don't believe so.' She released a shaky breath. 'I'd had backache all morning and if I hadn't done the pregnancy test I would just have assumed that my period had started late.'

Jace raked his fingers through his hair. His logical brain told him he should feel relieved that Eleanor was not pregnant, but he was thrown off-guard by her latest revelation. Why had he been so eager to seize the excuse of a baby to alter the terms of their marriage? Was it because he *wanted* to remain married to Eleanor?

Rocked by this astounding thought, he stared at her lovely face and felt his heart contract when he saw tears in her eyes. He wanted to take her in his arms and hold her, comfort her, but he instinctively knew she did not want that from him. The damning document that he'd forgotten about these past months had driven a chasm between them and he did not know how to bridge it.

'How do you feel about…?' He balked at saying *the failed pregnancy* or *the baby*, when there was no baby, and settled for, 'The situation?'

'I didn't believe I could be pregnant. The test result was a big shock,' she said in a choked voice. 'I hadn't got my head around the idea of having a baby, but then I wasn't.'

Jace watched her close the zip on the suitcase. She lifted the case off the bed, and he put his hand on her arm. 'I realise that you are upset,' he said carefully. 'But don't be too hasty to dismiss what we have, *matia mou*.'

She shook her head so that her dark blonde hair swirled around her shoulders in a fragrant cloud and Jace's body clenched.

'We don't have anything. Sure, the sex is great—' she stalled him before he could argue '—but it's not enough for me. My very brief pregnancy made me realise that I was wrong to marry you. I was desperate to save my brother from prison, but the truth is that Mark has to seek professional help for his gambling addiction, and save himself. I love him, but I'm not responsible for him.'

Jace was startled by Eleanor's serious tone and dropped his hand, allowing her to move away from him. 'You said that our marriage is not enough for you, so what do you want?' he asked gruffly.

'Love.' She met his frown with a rueful smile. 'The one thing you will never feel for me because I am Kostas Pangalos's granddaughter. But I deserve to be loved for *me*,' she said with fierce pride. 'Not held to account for a feud that happened when I was a child. I want to fall in love with a man who truly loves me. I want to stand in a church with him and proclaim our love in front of family and friends. And one day I hope that a positive result on a pregnancy test will fill me with joy rather than dread.'

'You're upset about losing the baby?'

She nodded. 'But it wouldn't have worked,

both of us stuck in an unhappy marriage for the sake of our child.'

Jace watched her walk across the room and felt sick in the pit of his stomach when he realised that she actually meant it, and she was leaving him. Did she think he would chase after her, or beg her not to go? His jaw hardened. He did not need her. He had never needed any woman.

'Where will you go?' he demanded. Call her bluff, he thought grimly, and see how quickly she backtracked.

'I've arranged to stay at an apartment in Thessaloniki. It's near to the hospice so that I can go with you to visit your mother. I suggest we don't tell her that we have broken up. She was so happy at the wedding and there is no need to upset her for the time she has left.'

'Clearly you have thought this out,' he drawled, glad of the white heat of his temper. But inside he felt icy-cold. 'What about your responsibilities managing the hotel?'

'I've asked the deputy manager to stand in for me. Ultimately, I expect you will want to appoint a manager to work alongside you, as…as we used to do' Her voice shook, but she quickly recovered. She halted next to the dressing table and took a pen out of her handbag, scrawled something on a piece of paper and held it out to him.

Jace took it and his heart crashed into his ribs as he stared at Eleanor's signature on the original prenuptial agreement which gave him one hundred per cent ownership of the Pangalos. 'What are you doing?'

'I'm giving you the only thing you really want.' Her sad smile wrecked him. 'You've won, Jace.'

CHAPTER TEN

'*TI KANEIS,* MAMÁ?' Jace murmured as he leaned over the bed and kissed his mother's cheek. Every day he asked her how she was, but every day she looked thinner and frailer and his eyes told him that her life was fading.

Iliana's eyes fluttered open and she smiled. 'I wasn't expecting you. Eleanor said that you were working late.'

'I came here straight from the office.' He did not admit that he put off returning to his empty house until as late as possible every evening. He had left the villa at the Pangalos resort the day after Eleanor had called time on their marriage. In Thessaloniki he was closer to the hospice where his mother was being cared for by the excellent staff.

On previous days Eleanor had met him in the hospice's car park, and they had visited his mother together. Somehow, they had put on a show of being lovestruck newlyweds, but he'd felt Eleanor's fingers tremble when he held her hand like lovers did, and when she had leaned close to him and rested her head on his shoulder he'd been unable to control his pounding heart.

Jace had assured himself that if he gave her space she would see sense and want to resume their marriage. He'd had several erotic fantasies in which Eleanor tried to persuade him to take her back. Invariably this had involved her taking her clothes off and begging him to make love to her, and of course he had relented and taken her to bed because sex with her was the best he'd ever had.

He bent his head towards his mother to catch what she was saying. 'You just missed your wife. She told me she was going home to cook your favourite dinner.'

Jace appreciated Eleanor's tactful lie. Memories swamped his mind of when they had prepared evening meals together at the villa on Sithonia. His culinary skills stopped at omelettes, but Eleanor enjoyed cooking and she had pottered about the kitchen, stirring ingredients in various saucepans, or stepped into the garden to pick fresh herbs for a salad dressing while he sat on a stool, drinking a glass of good red wine and slicing up tomatoes or zucchini when required.

And they had talked—about issues at the hotel, ideas for his property development business, a film they'd watched the previous night. He missed the easy companionship they'd shared. Hell, he missed *her*.

'Eleanor is a lovely girl with a kind heart,' his mother murmured. 'Kostas's granddaughter does not take after him.'

Jace stiffened. His mother's voice was weak, and he wondered if he had heard her correctly. 'How did you find out?'

She gave him a gentle smile. 'I recognised her on that first evening when you brought her to the house during the storm. There was a photograph of Kostas's family in the newspaper when he died. I believe it was a surprise that he had put Eleanor in charge of his hotel business.'

Jace let out his breath slowly. 'I didn't tell you who Eleanor was because I thought you might be upset that I had married the granddaughter of the man responsible for my father's death.'

'Eleanor cannot be held responsible for Kostas's actions.' Iliana closed her eyes and Jace thought she had fallen asleep, but then she said softly, 'I have been thinking about what happened to Dimitri.'

'Don't upset yourself,' Jace urged. 'Nothing can change the past.'

'But my perception of events has changed. Your father loved me, and he adored you. We tried for many years to have a child, and when you were born Dimitri wept tears of joy as he held his son in his arms.'

Iliana's eyes flew open and she said in a stronger voice, 'Your father would not have chosen to leave you, Jace. It is true that he was devastated when his best friend betrayed him. For a long time I blamed Kostas. But I believe in my heart that Dimitri fell to his death by accident. His eyesight was poor, and many times I warned him against walking on the clifftop.'

Jace felt a lump in his throat when he saw a tear trickle down his mother's sallow cheek. She held out her bony hand and he carefully clasped her fingers. Her breathing was shallow. Her gaze held his, and her tender smile was weary. 'Your father loved you,' she whispered. 'Dimitri was the love of my life and he would be as glad as I am that you have found your for ever love with Eleanor.'

'Thank you for coming,' Jace said brusquely to Eleanor when the last of the mourners who had attended his mother's funeral departed. He had organised a small gathering of close friends at the house after the service to commemorate Iliana's life. It had struck him that he was the last Zagorakis. Neither he nor his parents had had siblings, and the only distant relative of his father had died a few months ago.

'I was glad to come,' she said quietly. 'I was fond of your mother.' She hesitated. 'It's a sad day and I didn't want you to go through it alone.' She turned away from him, murmuring that she had left her jacket in the orangery.

Jace watched her walk away from him and his jaw clenched. *Alone.* The truth was that he could be in a roomful of friends and feel alone. A yawning chasm had opened up inside him in the two weeks since he'd stood by and allowed Eleanor to walk out of the villa. He told himself that he could not have prevented her from leaving. He couldn't give her the fairy tale she longed for. But the idea that she might be looking for love, and maybe she'd already met Mr Right, kept Jace awake at night. He had put his inability to sleep, eat or function in any meaningful way down to grief for his mother. Or it could simply be sexual frustration, he thought with grim self-derision.

Today was the first time he had seen Eleanor since his mother had died peacefully in her sleep a week ago. She looked elegant and stunningly beautiful in a silk shift dress that couldn't make up its mind if it were green or hazel—the same as her eyes. In front of the guests they had continued with the pretence of being happily married. Except that it hadn't been pretence, Jace brooded. He had felt the happiest he had ever been when Eleanor had shared his life. And he was fairly sure that she had been happy too. Why hadn't it been enough for her? Why did women always want more?

Why was he running away from the best

thing that had ever happened to him? Jace's heart slammed into his ribs as he was finally honest with himself. Eleanor had signed the Pangalos over to him, and before he had met her last year he would have sworn that the hotel was everything he desired. But he could not laugh with a hotel, or talk to a hotel. He had been driven to claim the Pangalos by a desire for vengeance. Now all he cared about was claiming the only person who understood him—his wife.

She must be out of her mind, Eleanor thought as she stepped into the master bedroom. What she was doing defied common sense, but her heart ached as she remembered Jace's sombre expression when his mother's coffin had been lowered into the grave. He was hurting. Oh, he hid it well, and at the reception after the funeral he had been his urbane and charming self. But she knew it had been an act. Jace Zagorakis, self-made multimillionaire with a playboy reputation and more friends than there were stars in the sky, had looked utterly alone.

No doubt he would say it was how he liked

to live his life. A lone wolf without emotional commitments, without emotions. But Eleanor was not fooled. He had loved his parents, who were now both dead. He cared deeply for his close friend Takis, who had been at the funeral, looking grimmer and more unsmiling than ever.

Jace had the capacity to love and it broke her heart that he would never love her. But he needed her tonight. Her fingers shook as she ran the zip on her dress down and the silk shift slithered to the floor. After a second's hesitation, she unclipped her bra, tugged off her knickers and slipped beneath the sheets. The shutters at the window were open, and the moonlight cast a pearly glow into the room and over the bed.

The bedroom door swung open and she heard Jace expel a ragged breath. He lounged in the doorway, as tall as a giant, his muscular body silhouetted against the light in the hallway.

'Well, well…' he drawled.

'I don't want to talk,' she said fiercely.

He gave a rough laugh as he walked into the room and closed the door behind him.

'Talking is not at the top of my list either.' His hand moved to his belt as he approached the bed. Eleanor's gaze locked with his, and the chemistry that had always simmered between them blazed. She shifted position so that she was kneeling on the mattress and slowly lowered the sheet.

The air felt cool on her naked breasts and her nipples hardened and jutted provocatively forwards. Jace made a low growl when she cupped her breasts in her palms before skimming her hands lower to the vee of tight curls at the junction of her thighs. It was empowering to play the temptress, and the feral gleam in his eyes as he halted next to the bed evoked a flood of sticky warmth between her legs. With a sultry smile, she slid her finger into her feminine heat and saw his eyes darken as he watched her pleasure herself.

'Witch,' he said thickly. 'Are you sure…?'

'I said no talking.' He would never say the words she longed to hear, and she could not tell him how she felt about him. But tonight she would show him with her body the secret she held in her heart. Tonight she would make sure that he never forgot her.

She undid the buttons on his shirt and pushed it off his shoulders, running her hands over his bunched biceps before moving to his chest and exploring the defined ridges of his muscular physique. His skin was warm satin beneath her fingertips, the whorls of black chest hair slightly abrasive against her palms. She followed the arrowing of hair down to the waistband of his trousers and unzipped him, deliberately brushing her hand over the bulge of his arousal.

He bent his head and pressed his mouth to her neck, trailed hot kisses along her collar-bone and moved down to her breasts, laving each pebble-hard nipple in turn until she trembled with need. Eleanor cupped her hands around his face and dragged his mouth up to hers. The kiss exploded between them, wild yet sweet, a sensual feast as their tongues tangled.

Jace stripped off the rest of his clothes and she pulled him down on top of her, spreading her legs so that his hard shaft pressed against her opening.

'I want you now. I can't wait,' she told him urgently. He made a harsh sound in his throat and lowered himself onto her, easing his erection deep inside her. It was bliss after two weeks without him and Eleanor moaned softly when he drew back and thrust slowly into her again, filling her, completing her. She speared her fingers into his hair and pressed her face against his throat, licking the slight saltiness of his skin before she nipped him with her teeth.

His primal groan of desire sent a shiver of feminine triumph through her. She pushed him off her, and when he rolled onto his back she straddled him and took his thick length inside her.

'You are incredible, *omorfiá mou,*' he rasped as she rolled her hips to meet his powerful thrusts and the rhythm became faster, harder until they soared together to a place of exquisite pleasure that was uniquely theirs.

For a long time afterwards, Eleanor did not move while she stored every detail, every sensation of Jace's lovemaking in her mind. The steady rise and fall of his chest told her that he had fallen asleep. Moonlight highlighted the sharp edges of his cheekbones and the sensual curve of his mouth. His eyelashes made dark crescents on his skin. In sleep he looked younger and she glimpsed the boy beneath the man.

'Goodbye,' she whispered against his lips. 'I will always love you.'

Jace woke to the pale light of dawn and for a moment he wondered if he had dreamed, as he so often did, of Eleanor. The languorous ache in his muscles told him that she had been real and not a figment of his imagination. She had seduced him and made love to him with an unguarded passion and he felt disappointed, but not surprised, that she had gone.

He reached for his phone and called the security team he'd tasked to ensure her safety. Not because he wanted to stifle her independence, but for his peace of mind, needing to know that no harm would come to her. After a brief conversation he ascertained that Eleanor had arrived back at her apartment late the previous night, and she had left again in her car half an hour ago. Jace had a good idea where she was heading, and he strode into the bathroom to shower, determined that he would not let her go again.

Unless she wanted her freedom. He felt the sensation of a lead weight dropping into the pit of his stomach, knowing that he had no right to keep her in a marriage that he'd insisted on for all the wrong reasons. Guilt cramped in his gut. And something else. Fear. What if he was too late to finally recognise the true reason why he had wanted Eleanor to be his wife?

He stared at his face in the mirror and grimaced as he ran his hand over the stubble on his jaw. His eyes looking back at him were dull, their bleak expression reflecting how he felt when he imagined a future without Eleanor. It would be nothing more than he deserved, he acknowledged. But he was hanging onto hope. It was all he had. A whispered promise against his lips that he might have dreamt, but perhaps had been real. There was only one way to find out.

The sliding glass doors in the bedroom at the villa on the Pangalos resort were open. The view of the turquoise pool and the sea beyond it was spectacular, but Jace's gaze was fixed on Eleanor. She was sitting at the top of the pool's stone steps and had her back to him.

He felt a tug in his chest as he paused and drank in the sight of her in a skimpy bikini, remembering how she used to cover up her body because she'd felt self-conscious about her scoliosis scar. When he walked noiselessly across the terrace he noticed a new mark on her back, close to her scar, and saw that it was a delicately inscribed tattoo. Just one word: *Warrior.*

She heard his footsteps and jerked her head in his direction, a wealth of emotion in her eyes before her lashes swept down, and Jace sensed that she was hastily erecting her defences.

'Did you know I would be here?'

'Of course I knew. I know everything about you, *matia mou,*' Jace said softly. 'You have no secrets from me.'

A blush spread over her face and she looked away from him. 'Why did you come after me?'

'Did you imagine I wouldn't, after what we shared last night?'

'We had sex.'

He was tempted to argue that it had been so much more, but he let it go for now. 'I like this,' he murmured, tracing his finger over her tattoo.

She gave a faint sigh. 'You taught me to be unafraid and to accept myself.'

His heart contracted. 'You were a warrior long before we met,' he said gruffly. 'Will you come inside? There are things we need to discuss.'

'Like what? I won't contest the divorce, and I've given you the Pangalos. What else is there to talk about?'

'Please.'

'Fine,' she muttered, ignoring his hand that he held out to help her to her feet. She jumped up and marched into the villa through the French windows that led into the sitting room. Arms folded defensively in front of her chest, she stared at him mutinously. 'Well?'

Eleanor wished that Jace would stop staring at her with an intent expression in his eyes that made her foolish heart tremble. Why didn't he just give her the divorce paperwork to sign, which was the reason she assumed he was here? She had managed to hold herself together driving from Thessaloniki to Sithonia, but tears were perilously near the surface.

She hadn't expected to see him again after she'd left him asleep last night, and this was pure torture. Typically, he looked amazing in faded jeans and a cream shirt with the sleeves rolled up to his elbows, revealing his tanned forearms thickly covered with black hair. Arms that would never hold her again.

He moved to the coffee table and took some papers out of his briefcase.

'Give me a pen and I'll sign the divorce application,' she said curtly. But when she skimmed her eyes over the documents she discovered that they were the two versions of the prenuptial agreement, one of which she had signed before she'd married Jace. The other was the original agreement that she had been unaware of until she'd signed it two weeks ago and forfeited her share of the hotel.

Jace took both documents from her and ripped them into tiny pieces, which fluttered to the floor in a mockery of the confetti that had been thrown at their wedding.

'I don't understand,' she said shakily.

'I hope this will explain.' He handed her another document and Eleanor caught her breath when she read it.

'Is this a joke? It says that you rescind all rights to the Pangalos Beach Resort, and I have sole ownership.'

He nodded. 'To make things absolutely clear, I have suggested calling the hotel by a new name.'

'Eleanor's Hotel.' She read the new name out. 'But...you married me for the hotel. My grandfather cheated your father out of his share.' Eleanor bit her lip. 'I don't want a hotel that is tainted by so much bitterness.' She thrust the new document at Jace. 'Keep it. I know how much the Pangalos means to you.'

'It means nothing to me,' he said savagely. 'There is only one thing—one person I care about.' Raw emotion thickened his voice. 'And that is you, *pouláki mou.*'

'Don't.' It was too cruel to offer her a dream when she was certain he would tear it down again.

He gave a wry smile. 'Are you asking me not to call you my little bird, or not to care about you?'

She shook her head, determined not to drown in his liquid gaze. 'Don't tell me any more lies. That's all I ask.'

'That's it, though. You have never asked for anything. Even the money you needed from me was to help your brother. I took advantage of your generous heart,' Jace said seriously, no smile on his lips now and an expression of uncertainty in his eyes that shook Eleanor. Jace Zagorakis—*uncertain*. It wasn't possible; he was the most self-assured man she had ever met. But a nerve flickered in his jaw and his tension was tangible when he picked up a box from the table and gave it to her. 'Open it.'

Mystified, she opened the lid and lifted out a little wooden carving of a sparrow. It was exquisite, and had been carved with such detail that each individual feather was perfect. 'Oh! How beautiful!' she murmured.

'Yes.' Jace was looking at her, not the carving, and Eleanor's heart missed a beat. 'Do you remember in Africa, we visited the Maasai tribe and one of the elders had carved various animals and birds? I asked him to make the carving. The elder said that the little sparrow does not seek attention like many of its colourful cousins, but a wise man knows that it is the bravest and most beautiful of all the birds.'

Jace's mouth twisted. 'I am not wise; I'm a fool. I ignored what my heart was telling me since before we went to Paris.'

She stiffened and placed the carving on the table. 'I was the fool to believe that you felt the same way about me as I did for you. In my defence, you were a very convincing fiancé and I was totally taken in by you. But in the back of my mind I wondered why you never mentioned love.' She shrugged. 'It became clear when I overheard your phone call with Takis, telling him that you were not in love with me.'

'That's what I told myself.' Jace raked his hand through his hair and took a jerky step towards her. 'I've never told you that I found my father at the bottom of the cliff. His injuries were horrific, but he was still alive—just.'

'Jace, don't,' Eleanor pleaded. The pain he clearly felt as he relived the terrible memory tore at her heart.

He closed his eyes briefly. 'I need to explain why I treated you so badly. My father made me promise that I would take care of my mother and reclaim the hotel for her. I was fifteen and I swore as I held my father's broken body that I would take vengeance on Kostas Pangalos.'

'Jace…' she pressed her knuckles against her mouth to hold back a sob '…it's over. The Pangalos is yours.'

'I don't want it.' He cupped her cheek in his hand, a hand that was as unsteady as the erratic thud of Eleanor's pulse. 'I want you to be my wife till death do us part, as we promised each other when we married.'

She stared at him, unable to believe what she was hearing. He stared back at her and she was afraid to trust what his night-dark eyes seemed to be telling her.

'*Why*, Jace? We made your mother happy before she died, and you have honoured the promise you made to your father. There is no reason for us to stay married.'

'There's this,' he said raggedly before he pulled her into his arms and lowered his head, claiming her mouth in a devastating kiss that sent her defences tumbling. He kissed her with fierce passion and such aching tenderness that she could not resist him. She felt the thunder of his heart when she laid her hand on his chest. Gone was the coolly controlled Jace who, even in the wildest moments of passion, had kept something back from her.

Now he kissed her as if he were a starving man and she was a feast. His big body shook as he crushed her to him, and his lips moved from her mouth, over her cheeks, the tip of her nose and claimed her lips again with a desperation that made her tremble.

At last he lifted his head and her breath snagged in her throat when she saw that his eyelashes were wet. 'I love you.'

Eleanor swallowed. 'Before…' she meant when he had courted her in England '… I would have given the earth to hear you say those words to me.'

'Does that mean you no longer want me to tell you that my heart is yours for as long as I live?' he said tautly.

'Only say it if it's true.'

His throat worked. 'I deserve your mistrust, but please believe me, *agapi mou*. I love you more than I knew it was possible to love. I fell in love with you that first week we spent together on the boat cruising around the islands. It's true,' he said deeply when she looked doubtful. 'But I couldn't admit how I felt. It seemed like a betrayal of the promise I had made to my father if I fell in love with Kostas's granddaughter.'

'That's just it,' Eleanor choked. 'I can't change who I am, and the bitterness you feel for my grandfather will always come between us.'

Jace brought his other hand up to cradle her cheek. 'I don't want to change anything about you, my angel. I love you because you are *you*. Beautiful and courageous, and with a depth of compassion that humbles me.'

He sighed. 'I used guilt as an excuse not to tell you how I felt about you. The truth is that I was devastated when my father died, and I saw that my mother was heartbroken. I never wanted to fall in love and risk the pain of loss.'

He smoothed her hair back from her face. 'Prison was hell, and soon after I was released I met Katerina and fell hard for her. When she made it clear that I wasn't good enough for her, I resolved never to put my heart on the line again. But then I met you, and you fell in love with me. You gave your love freely and bravely, even though you had suffered loss when your parents died. But I was a coward, and scared to admit to myself that I loved you beyond reason.'

Jace hesitated. 'Did I dream that last night you made love to me with love in your heart?'

Slowly she shook her head, trying to summon the courage to take a leap of faith. 'You didn't dream it.'

His gentle smile stole her breath. 'It was *never* just sex. Every time we made love, I told you with my body what my stubborn brain refused to accept. You are my world, Eleanor, and I have discovered these past weeks that the world is a dark and lonely place without you.'

He stared at her with eyes that were suddenly bleak when she did not respond. 'Will you give me another chance, *pouláki mou*, and allow me to try to win your love again? I swear I will prove that I truly love you with all my heart and soul, with everything that I am. Yours for eternity.'

Finally, Eleanor believed him, and happiness exploded inside her. 'I never stopped loving you,' she said softly. 'Even when I told myself that I hated you, I was hopelessly in love with you. Why else do you think I agreed to a marriage of convenience? It was my chance to try and win your love. But when I thought you had betrayed me again it felt that all hope had gone, especially as I had lost the baby who would have been a link between us.'

Jace groaned. 'I'm sorry I hurt you.'

She pressed her finger against his lips. 'Let's make a pact to leave the past behind and look to the future.'

He drew her close, and she curled her arms around his neck and laid her head on his chest, entranced by the urgent thud of his heart that echoed her own. For timeless moments they simply stood there, wrapped in each other's arms while love enfolded them. And then Jace kissed her, and it felt new and wonderful because now Eleanor knew there was love in his tender caresses. He claimed her lips with sensual passion and the fire that was always between them blazed.

'*Se agapó, kardiá mou,*' he said thickly as he carried her into the bedroom and tumbled them down on the bed. Her bikini, his clothes, were hurriedly removed, and their naked limbs entwined. 'You do realise that I plan to spend the foreseeable future making love to you?' Jace murmured as he positioned himself over her.

Eleanor gave him a joyous smile. 'I can't wait for our future together to begin.'

'It begins now, my love.'

EPILOGUE

THE HOT-AIR BALLOON rose gently into the blue sky. Below was the breathtaking scenery of the Meteora, a landscape dotted with huge monoliths and towering rock formations, on top of which several Greek monasteries clung perilously. The distant mountains were capped with snow that glinted in the golden sunrise.

Eleanor shut off the burner and turned to Jace. 'Isn't this amazing? I'm glad you came. You seem more relaxed in the balloon now.'

He grinned. 'I trust my pilot.'

She thought her heart might burst with happiness. 'I trust my co-pilot,' she said softly.

'I will never give you cause to doubt me.' He moved closer to her in the balloon basket and dropped down onto one knee. Eleanor's eyes widened when Jace took a square box out of his pocket and opened it. Inside was an exquisite engagement ring: a light blue sapphire surrounded by small diamonds that sparkled as brightly as the snow on the mountains. The delicate beauty of the ring brought a lump to her throat.

'You already gave me an engagement ring,' she murmured, feeling guilty that she was not wearing the huge diamond solitaire.

'I thought you would be impressed if I gave you a flashy, expensive ring, but I should have known that you do not value something by how much it cost. This suits you much better,' Jace said as he slid the pretty ring onto her finger, next to her wedding band. The sapphire was the clear blue of the sky.

'The ring is perfect, thank you.' Eleanor hesitated. 'Would you mind if I donated the diamond solitaire to the Scoliosis Support charity? They are holding an auction to raise money which will be used to give children with scoliosis some fun experiences, like I had when I was introduced to ballooning.'

Jace stood up and kissed the tip of her nose. 'I think it's a great idea. And, speaking of ideas, what do you think of having a ceremony to renew our wedding vows? I want to stand with you in front of family and friends and proclaim our love for each other.' He smiled, seeing that she remembered what she had said to him before she'd walked out of their marriage.

She nodded eagerly. 'I'm sure my brother would come, and bring his new fiancée. It will be lovely to meet Joanne. Mark seems to have put his problems behind him now that he's busy working with the horses on her family's stud farm in Ireland.' With a faint frown, she said, 'I might also get a chance to find out what's wrong with my sister. Lissa has seemed unhappy lately. When I told her that I've arranged with the bank for her to have full access to her trust fund, she burst into tears. Will you invite Takis?'

Jace nodded. 'I have already mentioned to him that we might want to hold the ceremony and reception at Eleanor's Hotel.'

'I think I would prefer to have it somewhere else. Even though the hotel's name has changed, I'll always think of it as the Pangalos, with its history of the feud between our families. I'm glad we sold the hotel to Takis. It's a fresh start for us.'

'You haven't told me yet if you are going to accept a position at Zagorakis Estates. We work well together.'

Eleanor took a deep breath. 'I would like to work alongside you in the future. I think we should renew our vows soon, while I can still fit into my wedding dress.' She gave Jace a tremulous smile. 'I've been feeling a bit nauseous recently. I didn't mention it because I didn't want you to worry,' she said quickly when he frowned. 'Anyway, the doctor sent me for an ultrasound scan, and... I'm still pregnant.'

Jace stared at her. '*Still* pregnant?'

'The doctor said it's likely that I conceived twins three months ago, and miscarried one of them. But the other baby is absolutely fine. I...we...are expecting a little girl.'

'*Theos!*' Jace looked stunned.

'You are pleased, aren't you?'

The expression of pride and pleasure in his eyes convinced her. 'My angel. How could you doubt it? Of course I'm pleased. I'm over the moon,' Jace assured her huskily. 'I'm the luckiest man in the world.'

* * *

Five and a half months later Eleanor gave birth to a healthy daughter. Jace was with her throughout her labour and his eyes glistened when he cradled the infant in his arms.

He sat on the edge of the hospital bed and kissed Eleanor tenderly. 'I love you. And I love our baby girl. Now we are a family.'

She gave him a tired but joyful smile. 'I love you too. Family sounds nice. But our baby needs a name.'

'Your middle name is Rose, and my mother's middle name was Acacia. What do you think of calling her Acacia Rose?'

'I think it's perfect.'

Jace looked down at the baby's tiny face, peeping out from the shawl she was swaddled in. He marvelled at her exquisite features. 'Our daughter is as beautiful as her mother,' he said softly. His heart was full. Love, family and a future that looked shining bright. 'Everything is perfect.'

* * * * *

LET'S TALK
Romance

For exclusive extracts, competitions
and special offers, find us online:

f facebook.com/millsandboon

◎ @millsandboonuk

🐦 @millsandboon

Or get in touch on 0844 844 1351*

For all the latest titles coming soon,
visit millsandboon.co.uk/nextmonth

*Calls cost 7p per minute plus your phone company's price per
minute access charge